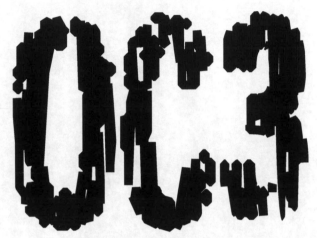

The Fate
Paradox

BRANDON S. TODD

 www.trafford.com

North America & international
toll-free: 1 888 232 4444 (USA & Canada)
fax: 812 355 4082

Dedicated To:
'Stan Lee'
'Aunt Cheryl'
And 'Popaw Joe'

PREAMBLE:

ARTICLE I. <u>THE ORGANIZED CHAOS THEORY</u>

The world is in a state of chaos as the power structure of the world is meeting its demise. The political, economic, governmental, societal, religious, etc. structures of the world are rotting, collapsing, and crumbling before our eyes. Chaos is prominent throughout all the Earth, as war, poverty, mass shootings, terrorism, and Orwellian spying are manifesting all across America and the world.

The United States itself is in a state of degradation and chaos, while nationalism, corporatism, communism, and totalitarianism are reemerging throughout the globe. Politicians don't have a clue what to do to rescue the nation or the world for that matter. The American People are unwilling to take matters in their own hands and contain the chaos, and as a result the economy, our society, and everything in between are being corrupted and taken hostage by tyrannical forces.

However, the chaos that is spreading throughout the world is not spontaneous. We are experiencing Organized Chaos of epic proportions. The system has been rigged, and the people of the world are being enslaved by the nefarious forces taking hold of the institutions and systems around the globe. They are overtaking every institution known to man, and they are perpetrating chaos.

It is insane how the American people have allowed the select few in power to take control over their lives and their country. Every action has an equal and opposite reaction. As a result of the tyranny in America, we will experience revolution. As a result of the corruption by our government, we are waking up and questioning the government's authority and the government is losing its power. The American people, and the citizens of the world, are regaining their power.

The minorities of America and the World are becoming the majority, and by God, things in this world are going to change for the better and for the worse.

The chaos we are witnessing on the world stage is not random. The world, and its institutions, are being manipulated and controlled, much like the chaos taking place. The organized chaos taking place cannot be denied, nor can it be ignored.

The world is a place of organized chaos. The Universe, and everything in between, was birthed out of chaos. As human beings, we are made in God's image, and we can transform entropy into order. We can organize chaos as well. Without government, politics, military, economics, religion, school, etc. we as human beings would be living in a state of complete and utter chaos. However, we are able to organize ourselves and manipulate the chaos to meet our needs within communities, families, societies, and cultures. Human beings organize chaos. If we didn't control the chaos, we would be consumed by Nature.

The world is ruled by Natural Law. The governing dynamics with which we govern are dictated by Natural Law, especially here in America. Our constitution is a creation of organized chaos based upon natural law. It is a document that was formulated to provide a structure for the American People and our rights. Without it we would have complete chaos. With it, our country, society, economy, and institutions are organized, protected, and respected. Our gift as human beings is, we can take the ordinary and turn it into the extraordinary. We can take war and turn it into peace. We can take darkness and turn it into light.

The organized chaos of the world is needed. Everything is in a state of chaos; always has been, always will be. But, it is our duty as human beings to unify, organize, and free ourselves from total and all-out chaos. I've come to learn that organized chaos is better than pure chaos; but, even pure chaos is organized in some way, shape or form. Democracy tends to Anarchy. Order tends to disorder.

The comedic genius, Steve Martin once stated: "Chaos in the midst of chaos isn't funny, but chaos in the midst of order is." I couldn't agree more. As human beings, a lot of us almost crave chaos. More specifically, most people crave organized chaos. Truthfully, we get bored and chaos brings us back to life. It gives an adrenaline-rush and a thrill; a jolt to the soul, if you will.

Chaos makes the world go round.

In this world of maelstrom, societies, nations, empires fall, and more rise from the ashes. That is the natural order of things. Our sweet, precious America is collapsing as is the World. We must stop it before it's too late. The chaos must be contained. However, I must say myself that I prefer chaos over control.

On another note, we can't let politics prevent citizens from rising up and regaining control of America. As we, as human beings, are all political animals, I say it is time for us to take over the farm once more. It's time to save the Republic, and it is time to defeat the agents of chaos and totalitarianism that are threatening America and her interests.

The chaos is necessary. It is universal. Entropy, however drastic it may be, allows for order. Truth be told, we need chaos just as much as we need order in this world. However, chaos without order is a very dangerous thing. Order without chaos is false peace. We need true peace in this world, and the only way to achieve it is through organized chaos. Use the chaos to your advantage and use your power as an individual for the cause of good. I ask of you to stand up to your masters, and reclaim your authority as an individual.

The American People need to take back the nation from the hands of those in the shadows. We cannot allow the terrorists, communists, anarchists, jihadists, socialists, corporatists, fascists, nationalists, etc. to harm our nation or the world any longer. The American People and the citizens of the world must take their power back. We will take our power back. Don't be intimidated by the chaos. Embrace it. The chaos will always reign, and it's up to us as human beings to recognize that all chaos is, in one way or another, organized.

ARTICLE II: <u>THE CYBER WORLD WAR</u>

The Cyber World War is nearing. The Cold War II is merely a precursor to the Cyber World War; the war of the future. Eventually, wars will be fought strictly with machines; drones, robotic minions and cybernetic assassins. The Supercomputers of today's technological age will themselves create the sentient-Quantum computers of the next age. In hundreds of years computers and technology will transcend the universe, space and time.

Ultimately, machines will merge with man and the difference between man and machine will be indistinguishable. This is known as the Singularity. It is believed that the Singularity will be achieved late in the 21st century. If that happens, then cyberwarfare will manifest itself at a more rapid pace and broader scale than we are seeing now. Wars fought with men, guns and bullets will become obsolete.

I must pose some theoretical questions:

1. What if the Chinese deployed an army of cybernetic flies, carrying biological agents, to contaminate the water supplies of America?
2. What if the Russians developed the capability to hack American drones and perform an attack on a major US city?
3. What if the Iranians hit America with an EMP and then somehow sent nukes our way?

If it's plausible then it's possible. The threat of cyberwarfare is real and great. Cyber-espionage, a major component of cyberwarfare, has been occurring for the last two decades or more. Russian, Chinese, and Arab intelligence agencies and spies have penetrated, infiltrated and embedded themselves in America's businesses, universities, think-tanks and various other institutions.

America's enemies are many and they are committed to our demise as a country and a people. Therefore, it is up to the law enforcement, intelligence and national security agencies of our country to stand up and fight back against our foes; they must fight for America and defend the American People.

Norman Ralph Augustine once said: "One of the most feared expressions in modern times is, 'The Computer is down'." He wasn't kidding...

The Cyber World War is approaching. We must be prepared...

ARTICLE III: <u>COMMUNISM IS DEAD</u>

Communism has, and always will be, a cataclysmic catastrophe wherever exercised. In Communist countries throughout the past, the individual is nothing in comparison to 'The Party' or the regime. The Politburo and all its off-shoots were beyond totalitarian. Central Committees planned everything, from top to bottom; while ruling with Iron-Fists and giant imprisoning walls.

Communism today has only survived because regimes that implement it also practice capitalism economically. Politically, however? The way of Communism still exists; one party systems, oppressive and authoritarian by nature. Those regimes have maintained absolute political power, while also managing to make a buck or two.

Individualism in those places is nearly non-existent. People move as numbers, and work as such. No Bill of Rights will be found in Russia; at least not a legitimate one.

The Russians and the Chinese…they're only Communist because they've been forced fed to be so. Doctors, Lawyers, even Janitors, somehow, someway work for The State, The Party. Their elections are really rigged, opposition is not accepted, resistance is futile in those nations that practice Marx's ridiculous ideology.

Socialists across America are trying to revitalize Marx's ideas. However, I see them as a threat. Blinded by a manifesto that will wreak havoc. The end-game of Socialism is Communism. Be not deceived. Every Socialists true goal is, and will continue to be, the establishment of a Communist regime and society, here, anywhere.

If only American Socialists would truly examine the maniacal manifesto, only then would they see, it is really against their own interests.

If I had a quarter for every-time I've heard: "Jesus is a Communist", then I would be a very rich man indeed. Jesus was not a Communist. His consciousness was above ours, utterly. His ideology is the same. Stalin was a Communist. Mao Zedong was a Commie.

Jesus was The Son of God; a Divinely Holy Being, all Man, and all God. However, I'm here to tell you, Jesus was absolutely not a Communist. And, I don't think he'll be one when He is Risen. To put God in the same sentence as Communism, in my view, is Blasphemous.

Communism is against Private Property, the Family, the Upper and Middle classes; Marx claims in his writings that those things need to be 'abolished'. Now why would God support a ideology that calls for the complete abolition of Private Property and The Family; the eradication of the middle and upper classes? Beats me.

The extreme ideology, to me, is very cult-like; in writing and in practice. All those Communist Leaders of the past formulated themselves into 'Cult of Personalities', "purging" any and all in their way. Read any history book from after 1970 and you'll see that Communism is responsible for more death and devastation than the Bubonic Plague.

It's almost a religion. The incarnations of which have only sought to totally control their respective citizenries, ruthlessly, unrelentingly. It all boils down to control for any Communist Party in power. Their demagoguery doesn't match their actions, they never have in the history of the world.

All Communist regimes have committed an onslaught of horror because the utopian concept was run by men. Utopianism is not a good thing; perfection, when it comes to anything human, is corruption. Communism, foundationally, implies that government is naturally good, and it's not by a long shot.

Government, inherently, is not meant to protect people…it's meant to protect and ensure their rights. Government is not supposed to be good or bad, perfect or imperfect; it is merely supposed to preserve the liberties of The Individual. Liberties which by American standards are 'God-given'.

In systems that have practiced Socialism and/or Communism, the individual has been suffocated, downtrodden, put to the side. Communists, when in power, put their Party over all; and they'll use any means of force to maintain their self-fabricated order.

Governments become corrupt over time. Even Doctors get sick, you know? Governments become tyrannical if left unchecked. Communism in America is a paradox beyond words. Marx's way of governance is antithetical to Americanism.

I present some questions: What if Russia had defeated America during The Cold War? What would the world be like?

Hell is what it would be. Un-American Hell.

In every instance of history where Communism was truly applied, The State has trumped The Individual, and Natural Law has not been abided.

It's wholly unacceptable to me that there are many American Communists out there, studying Marx, thinking it's right.

If Commies get their way, there would be 100 percent taxation; no private property would be permitted.

You want my property? You want to abolish my Family? You'll have to do so over my cold-dead corpse. Communism has failed. I'm grateful to God that Communism is a relic.

More Power to The Individual, and his-or-her Rights.

<u>OC3: THE FATE PARADOX</u>

FADE IN:

INT. AGENT ORANGE'S MANSION - DAY

LOCATION: MIAMI

YEAR: 2016

THE MANSION is a product of its owner...orange walls
throughout...

The place is great in size, abstract in its design.

MOVERS are collecting and transporting AGENT KIMBO ORANGE's
belongings and possessions as he is dead, by the hands of
former DETECTIVE JOHN MARSHALL.

In his MANSION is a gilded cage containing a CROW; it is
perched, silently and patiently...

> MOVER 1
> --This guy has a fuck-ton of
> stuff, man.--

> MOVER 2
> -You mean 'DEAD-GUY'. But,
> No-shit. I don't know whether to
> move it or steal it...

> MOVER 1
> What about that CROW...in the
> cage.--

> MOVER 2
> We're definitely not taking it
> with us. LET IT FREE.

> MOVER 1
> --MIGHT AS WELL.--

MOVER 1 walks over to the gilded-cage, and frees the tamed
bird. MOVER 2 opens the window as to let it fly out.

Before exiting, THE CROW lands on the window-seal.

> THE CROW
> --Thank You, Gentlemen. Now--As
> You Were.

THE CROW flies off, full-speed-ahead.

                        MOVER 1
          --Did that bird just talk, or did
          you lace my coffee with acid
          again?

                        MOVER 2
                   (now moving stuff)
          --Don't sweat it, man. Crows have
          the best body-to-brain ratio.
          They're some of the smartest
          creatures on the earth, no doubt.
          It talked, yeah. They're smarter
          than humans...dolphins even.

                        MOVER 1
                   (helping move)
          Damn. That's intense, man.

                        MOVER 2
          --Yeah, it is.

                                        CUT TO:

EXT. THE COMINTURN HQ--MOSCOW - EVENING

                                        YEAR: 2021

The snowy landscape...

The blizzard is furious in RUSSIA.

The COMINTURN is almost not visible with the incessant
down-pour of flakes.

                                        CUT TO:

INT. THE COMINTURN HQ--RUSSIA - CONTINUOUS

A man, a scientist, stands prey to his superiors...to THE
COMINTURN. DR. VLADIMIR MILSTEIN is 61 years of age,
white-haired, tan-skinned, RUSSIAN to the core of his soul;
his hair is longer than expected for a doctor.

He has dark-brown eyes, a unibrow, and shadows of white and
black facial-hair.

                        DR. CHECKOV
          --We expect more, better results,
          now!!!

                    DR. ALINKOV
--Every experiment results in
failure with YOU, MILSTEIN!!!
Shall we Euthanize you
instead!!???

                    DR. VLADIMIR MILSTEIN
No--I simply---

                    PARTY LEADER/PREMIER
--If you speak unless asked to
again, I'll have your tongue
removed. Understood, Doctor?

                    DR. VLADIMIR MILSTEIN
Yes, Sir...

                    PARTY LEADER/PREMIER
Now, you will continue with what
progress you've made, until you
formulate a solution that provides
results. Until then, you stay
locked in the LAB, figuring how to
make the soldiers we need. The
Americans--they're working on this
very same program, SUPER-SOLDIERS.
I'm sending you there: NEW YORK
CITY to be exact. You will perfect
your research information, and you
yourself will continue the trials
and what not. You will move onto
human-trials, and you'll capture
Americans, see if the formula you
will develop works on their
senses. We must have these
soldiers with as many advantages
as possible!!! You will embed
yourself into LIFE-CONTROL, as
your deceased cousins, COTOMAN and
BRIAN WOLF, did. I need you to
replace them. You will do so, and
you'll give us our SUPER SOLDIERS,
or you will perish...your---OUR
achievements should leave our
enemies breathless. The clock is
ticking, Doctor...

                              CUT TO:

EXT. MOSCOW-AIRPORT - LATER

DR. VLADIMIR MILSTEIN waits in the snow for his plane's loading-gear to drop so that he may depart from his motherland to fulfill the needs of THE PARTY.

> DR. VLADIMIR MILSTEIN
> (narrating,
> getting on his
> plane)
> --COMMUNISM, a relic of the old MOTHER RUSSIA; my mother. I guess I am a relic myself, as I am one of the last true Communists alive, fighting for my country. My cousins---They were decent men, fighting for the homeland; true Communists too. I miss COTOMAN and BRIAN; wolves though they may be. I fucking hate the people who run my country. They're a bunch of idiots, taking orders from even bigger idiots. I get sick of it. Taking orders from them, to fulfill their stingy desires. I seek a broader horizon. There's no such thing as "applied sciences"...there's only the pure application of science itself. My goal is one that will ensure the evolution of the human race. And, I'm starting big. Not monkeys. NO. Dogs. Dogs are the key. The reward of a thing well done, is to have done it. MY MASTERS WANT RESULTS, I'll give 'em to 'em.---

MILSTEIN enters the plane, ready to go...to AMERICA.

> CUT TO:

EXT. ALLEY-WAY - MORNING

> ACT I. THE FEARLESS
> LITTLE-MAN AND
> FRIENDS

> LITTLE-MAN
> (narrating)
> --This is my story. I'm a dog, yeah, but I can talk--like you. I'm not special. I'm blessed and cursed.--More Blessed,
> (MORE)

> LITTLE-MAN (cont'd)
> however.---I've been through
> things that no man, or animal
> should ever be subjected to. But,
> I persevered. I'm what you would
> call gifted, and I use my gifts
> for good. I try to anyhow. To put
> it frankly, I watch over my City.
> New York. I'll do anything to
> protect it, the people in it, with
> all my might. The people and the
> dogs that I love, I'd give my life
> for them...even a stranger, it's
> all the same. I've always had this
> motivation since I was a pup.---

YEAR: 2021

LOCATION: NEW YORK
CITY

The vastness of NYC is met by its beauty. The skyscrapers stand tall, and the people walk fast, scurrying about their daily lives, jobs, and routines.

The city is a sight to behold. The stock market bell rings loudly, being heard from throughout the distance.

Police-sirens are roaring all around NYC, as cops and crooks battle it out. However, some in the Big Apple are at peace, resting...

4 Dogs lay in an ALLEY-WAY, fairly unseen in the shade. Many are walking the streets of New York City, however the ALLEY-WAY is a safe-place for the animals; not many humans pass by, nor do they bother the innocent, survivalist canines.

The Dogs are named KIMBA-SUE(Black and White), SAMPSON(All White), SCOOTER(Brown), and there is a puppy: LITTLE-BIT(White with shades of Brown and Gray). The pup is a newborn, only several weeks old...

KIMBA, a Shih-Tzu, is his mother. SAMPSON, an Osa-Lopsa, his father. SCOOTER, a Chihuahua, well, let's say he's his uncle.

This LITTLE-BIT, he becomes a LITTLE-MAN in the most magnificent way.

THIS STORY IS INSPIRED BY A DOG tougher and more brave THAN ANY MAN I'VE EVER MET...

                        KIMBA-SUE
                   (waking up, yawns)
              --Okay, everybody up. We gotta get
              breakfast--especially for
              LITTLE-BIT.

SAMPSON and SCOOTER awaken swiftly, LITTLE-BIT is still
snuggling with his newspaper.

KIMBA is the matriarch of their small family.

                        SAMPSON
                   (stretches)
              --What should we try to get today,
              KIMBA? Pizza? Or should I go to
              the Restaurant on 5th, and see
              what they got?--

The Dogs talk almost telepathically.

Humans cannot comprehend the dogs, but they do speak among
themselves.

                        UNCLE SCOOTER
                   (struggling to
                    wake up a bit)
              --If I must say, I'd like Chinese
              myself.

                        SAMPSON
              Chinese? For Breakfast?

                        KIMBA-SUE
              --I don't care what we eat, but we
              gotta eat, so get to it, boys.

                        UNCLE SCOOTER
              Yes, Ma'am.

                        SAMPSON
              I'm on it, dear.

SAMPSON and SCOOTER depart from the ALLEY-WAY.

LITTLE-MAN gently wakes up, and he immediately finds his
mother, and nurses.

She nurses him, but also gives him tastes of real food here
and there. She's transitioning him.

                        YOUNG LITTLE-MAN (LITTLE-BIT)
                   (finishes up
                    nursing KIMBA)
              Thank You, Mama. How are you
                        (MORE)

                    YOUNG LITTLE-MAN (LITTLE-BIT) (cont'd)
today?

          KIMBA-SUE
Well, my LITTLE-BIT, I'm doing
good. How about you, my sweet, how
are you?

          YOUNG LITTLE-MAN (LITTLE-BIT)
I feel like the "goodest"
LITTLE-MAN on the planet!

          KIMBA-SUE
--You'll be the best LITTLE-MAN
one day, in the universe. This I
know, my Son.--

          YOUNG LITTLE-MAN (LITTLE-BIT)
--Till then...I gotta pee, and
poop.--

          KIMBA-SUE
You gotta start somewhere, huh?

          YOUNG LITTLE-MAN (LITTLE-BIT)
Yes, Ma'am.

                              CUT TO:

EXT. CHINESE RESTAURANT - LATER

SAMPSON and SCOOTER approach a CHINESE RESTAURANT. They're
moving toward the back, unnoticed, unseen--like--NINJAS.

The Dogs aren't your average Dogs, let's put it that way.

They know how to scavenge to feed themselves. Whatever it
takes.

          SAMPSON
SCOOTER, you watch out for the
humans, I'll gather the loot.

          UNCLE SCOOTER
     (gives him a
      "paws-up")
You got it, brother-man.

          SAMPSON
Time to make shit happen.

                              CUT TO:

As SCOOTER keeps watch for SAMPSON, the Osa-Lopsa sprints to
the WASTEPRO dumpster in the back of the CHINESE RESTAURANT
and hits the mother-load.

When he sees the food, he is filled with pure excitement and
relief.

He quickly, and precisely, gathers the food: Sesame Chicken,
Rice, Shrimp, etc. SAMPSON puts it in bags and jumps out of
the WASTEPRO DUMPSTER with a couple of bags full of food.
SAMPSON is strong, and he's a good Dog; a good FATHER to his
pup and a good mate to KIMBA.

He gets the hell-out-dodge with the food.

He and SCOOTER, like bandits, take-off with a couple of
goodie-bags.

                    UNCLE SCOOTER
              (to SAMPSON,
               assists him as
               they run away)
          --You're a saint, and a scholar,
          SAMPSON.

As they run, SAMPSON hands SCOOTER one of the bags of food.

It's a like a bank-heist or something.

                    SAMPSON
          No sweat. We'll be good for a
          couple days off this load.

                    UNCLE SCOOTER
              (sprinting with a
               bag of food in
               his mouth)
          Yes, indeed, brother-man.

                              CUT TO:

INT. ALLEY-WAY - CONTINUOUS

LITTLE-BIT and KIMBA sit safely and securely in the
ALLEY-WAY, awaiting their food.

LITTLE-BIT, however, like any pup would, is getting bored.

                    YOUNG LITTLE-MAN (LITTLE-BIT)
          Will you read me one of my books,
          Mama, just to pass the time?

                    KIMBA-SUE
          You got it, buddy. Which one would
          you like me to read to you?

                    YOUNG LITTLE-MAN (LITTLE-BIT)
          Read 'The Amazing Spider-Man' to
          me.

                    KIMBA-SUE
          What is it with you and
          Spider-Man?

                    YOUNG LITTLE-MAN (LITTLE-BIT)
          --I like how he's from New York
          City, and how he saves it from all
          the bad-guys!--

LITTLE-BIT has a small collection of dirty, yet readable
Comic-Books...

He has 4 total: Spider-Man, Batman, Superman, and X-Men. His
mother KIMBA reads them to him quite a bit.

                    YOUNG LITTLE-MAN (LITTLE-BIT)
          --IF I GET THE CHANCE...I'M GOING
          TO SAVE THIS CITY ONE DAY, AND
          STOP THE BAD MEN.--

                    KIMBA-SUE
          --Son, you can do anything you put
          your mind to. ANYTHING. Now, go
          fetch your book, and I'll read to
          you till ya daddy gets back.

                    YOUNG LITTLE-MAN (LITTLE-BIT)
          Okay, Mama, awesome.

                                        CUT TO:

EXT. CITY STREET - CONTINUOUS

SCOOTER and SAMPSON walk the streets as people do, holding
their bags with great diligence, making sure the contents do
not spill.

They're moving at a good pace. Some of the people walking by
them smile and are awed, but most of them pay the dogs no
mind.

                    UNCLE SCOOTER
          --I call first-dibs on the Sesame
          Chicken.--

> SAMPSON
> --We gotta get there first, idiot.
> Just stay focused. You know we're
> near.

> UNCLE SCOOTER
> Yeah, yeah, yeah. I know. I'm just
> ravenous over here.

                                    CUT TO:

Suddenly, out-of-nowhere, an ANIMAL PATROL vehicle appears
about 30 yards ahead of SCOOTER and SAMPSON.

They stop dead in their tracks.

> SAMPSON
> (jukes, and evades
> sight from THE
> DOG CATCHER)
> Shit! Cut to the right, into the
> alley! We gotta take a detour!

They sprint with their bags-in-mouth, finding an alternate
route to avoid being detected.

THE DOG CATCHER will abduct any stray he sees. All the
strays have heard of him.

> UNCLE SCOOTER
> --What are we going to do? What if
> he saw us?!

> SAMPSON
> --He didn't. Don't worry. If he
> would've seen us, we'd be in cages
> right now.

                                    CUT TO:

EXT. ALLEY-WAY - LATER

LITTLE-BIT stands under his mother as she finishes up
reading to him.

She concludes the Spider-Man comic-book.

> YOUNG LITTLE-MAN (LITTLE-BIT)
> --Will you read it again? Please,
> Mama?

                    KIMBA-SUE
Son, give it a rest. I gotta eat
before anything. In fact, I can
smell ya daddy and UNCLE SCOOTER
coming now. They're about, uh--
          (raises her nose
           and sniffs)
--3 blocks away.

               YOUNG LITTLE-MAN (LITTLE-BIT)
Wow, I'm excited now. I wonder
what they're bringing back?

                    KIMBA-SUE
          (sniffs a little
           harder)
Chinese.

               YOUNG LITTLE-MAN (LITTLE-BIT)
How in the heck do you know that?

                    KIMBA-SUE
--Ya Mama's got a good-sniffer.
You will too as you keep growing.
It's gotta be developed with time
and practice.

               YOUNG LITTLE-MAN (LITTLE-BIT)
Yes, Ma'am.

                                   CUT TO:

EXT. ALLEY-WAY - MOMENTS LATER

SCOOTER and SAMPSON make their way around the corner with
the food safe and secure.

               YOUNG LITTLE-MAN (LITTLE-BIT)
     Hello, Papa and UNCLE SCOOTER!

                    SAMPSON
--Hey, there my little buddy. We
got you and your Mama some
goodies.

                    UNCLE SCOOTER
--LITTLE BIT, I swear up and down,
you've grown since we went to just
get the food. Boy, you're
sprouting like a wild-weed.

LITTLE-MAN bum-rushes his father and uncle, greeting them
with excitement. KIMBA stretches.

                    KIMBA-SUE
          Yes, he is, huh?

                    SAMPSON
          ----LITTLE-BIT, I got you a
          fortune-cookie, my dude.--

                    YOUNG LITTLE-MAN (LITTLE-BIT)
          --What's it say?

                    SAMPSON
               (gives him the
                fortune-cookie)
          --That's for you to find out.

The puppy opens the treat ever-so-quickly and consumes it
on-the-spot.

He then attempts to read the fortune...

                    YOUNG LITTLE-MAN (LITTLE-BIT)
               (stumbling a bit)
          A--A

His mother steps up to him and helps him read it.

                    KIMBA-SUE
          --"AWAKEN YOUR DIVINE NATURE
          WITHIN."--

                    YOUNG LITTLE-MAN (LITTLE-BIT)
          --What the heck does that mean,
          Mama?

                    KIMBA-SUE
          It means, KNOW THYSELF. BE
          THYSELF, my son. Now, let's pray
          and eat, I am famished.

At the utterance of those words, the 4 Dogs hear a vehicle
pull up at the entrance of the ALLEY-WAY.

All of them look to see who it is.

                    KIMBA-SUE
               (disturbed,
                unsettled)
          Oh, no.

                        SAMPSON
            KIMBA, SCOOTER! Get LITTLE-BIT out
            of here, now! I'll hold him off!

IT IS THE DOG CATCHER, of all people...

LITTLE-BIT is petrified, he starts to stand with his father,
but his mother forces him the other way.

                    THE DOG CATCHER
                    (exiting his
                     vehicle with a
                     tranquilzer-gun
                     in-hand)
            --Well, well. What do we have
            here? 4 Mutts, just what the
            DOCTOR ordered.

SAMPSON growls fiercely and charges THE DOG CATCHER...

The man shoots three darts into SAMPSON in a matter of
seconds.

He runs some more, but ultimately flops over, going
unconscious.

                    KIMBA-SUE
                    (stops and turns
                     around)
            --NO!

                YOUNG LITTLE-MAN (LITTLE-BIT)
                    (stunned)
            --Papa?

                    UNCLE SCOOTER
            KIMBA, there's nothing we can do,
            let's go!

The nefarious DOG CATCHER pulls out the BIG-GUN. He
shoots...

A giant net moves at the three dogs like a bullet, and it
ensnares them.

                    KIMBA-SUE
                    (fighting to break
                     free)
            --It'll be okay, LITTLE-BIT! Don't
            Be Afraid!

THE DOG CATCHER pulls yet another weapon and gasses
LITTLE-BIT, KIMBA, and SCOOTER, knocking them out

instantaneously.

The henchman loads the unconscious animals into the back of
his work-truck, in individual cages...

                    THE DOG CATCHER
                 (smiling with
                  villainy)
          THE EUTHANIZER will be very
          pleased...

THE DOG CATCHER speeds off from the ALLEY-WAY like a
bat-out-of-hell.

                              CUT TO:

EXT. THE LABORATORY - DAY

The dogs wake up as the truck parks...

SAMPSON does not. He was introduced to too much
tranquilizer.

                    KIMBA-SUE
          Is everybody all right?
          LITTLE-BIT? SCOOTER? SAMPSON?

                    YOUNG LITTLE-MAN (LITTLE-BIT)
          M-M-Mama?

                    KIMBA-SUE
          I'm here, son.

                    UNCLE SCOOTER
          I'm all right, KIMBA, I'm going to
          try to get us out of here. Hold
          on.

                    UNCLE SCOOTER
                 (biting at the
                  cage bars
                  unsuccessfully)
          SAMPSON?

                    KIMBA-SUE
                 (sniffs for
                  SAMPSON)
          --He can't be...He's dead...

                    UNCLE SCOOTER
          No...

THE DOG CATCHER and a couple of other HENCHMEN grab
LITTLE-BIT, KIMBA-SUE, and SCOOTER as they frantically try
to elope from the cages...

The men proceed to take the animals into DR. MILSTEIN'S LAB.

                    KIMBA-SUE
          LITTLE-BIT, whatever happens--Know
          that I will always Love You--I'll
          always be there for You.

                    YOUNG LITTLE-MAN (LITTLE-BIT)
               (trembling)
          Okay, Mama. I love you, too.

                    UNCLE SCOOTER
          LITTLE-BIT, you be good.

                    YOUNG LITTLE-MAN (LITTLE-BIT)
          --Yes, sir, UNCLE SCOOTER.--

The Dogs are separated as they're carried into the LAB.

                                        CUT TO:

INT. THE LAB HALL-H - MOMENTS LATER

SCOOTER and KIMBA, along with the corpse of SAMPSON, are
being taken to another side: HALL-E.

LITTLE-BIT is being taken down HALL-H by the DOG CATCHER.

It is a silent, depressing hall-way, a spine-tingling
silence is spread throughout the LAB-BUILDING.

LITTLE-BIT can actually read, he sees at the end of the
hallway, a sign that reads DR. VLADIMIR MILSTEIN.

The DOG CATCHER drops LITTLE-BIT in front of the door, and
knocks.

                    THE DOG CATCHER
               --Doc, I got those 4 like you
               asked. A pup and three other older
               ones.

                    DR. VLADIMIR MILSTEIN
               --Good, good. Thank You. The
               Elders---use them for dissection
               and trials...Leave the pup with
               me, and you leave from me.

24

                         THE DOG CATCHER
              --Yes, Sir.--

DR. MILSTEIN kneels down as to greet LITTLE-BIT.

                    DR. VLADIMIR MILSTEIN
                   (to LITTLE-BIT,
                    kind of friendly
                    in a odd way)
              --You and I, my LITTLE-friend, we
          have a lot of work to do.

MILSTEIN puts his hand to the cage, enveloping the
defenseless LITTLE-BIT in darkness.

                                        CUT TO:

INT. DR. MILSTEIN'S LAB - NIGHT

LITTLE-BIT is caged, isolated. MILSTEIN enters, to check on
the little dog.

                    DR. VLADIMIR MILSTEIN
               My Little Friend. How's your day
               going? I know, I know, you've been
               caged for three days straight.
               Well...You're about to be freed,
               so that I may experiment on you,
               freely.

                                        CUT TO:

                                        OVER THE COURSE OF 2
                                        YEARS

LITTLE-BIT is waterboarded. Yes, waterboarded.

The dog is electrocuted.

He is tranquilized.

Awakened.

The cycle repeats, and it is more than vicious.

We see THE EUTHANIZER, MILSTEIN, take out one of
LITTLE-BIT's eyes.

He tortures the animal, beyond measure...he does this, every
single day for 2 years...

                                        CUT TO:

INT. COP-CAR - NIGHT

                              YEAR: 2023

A middle-aged, black DETECTIVE, TRAVIS PARKER, is cruising
down a NYC STREET.

As he rides he proceeds to make a phone-call.

                    DETECTIVE TRAVIS PARKER
                 (talking into the
                  phone,
                  mid-discussion)
          --CHIEF, I don't know the full
          extent of what's about to happen.
          All I know, is the New York Mob
          and the Russian Mob are in
          conflict. My snitch tells me that
          the Russians are planning
          something big, and that they're
          using legitimate fronts for means
          of secret experimentation on
          animals and humans alike. My
          contact alluded to something along
          the lines of The Russians creating
          Super-Soldiers with Dog-DNA. And,
          and God I hope he's wrong, there's
          gonna be an attack in the city;
          they're hitting hard, sir, from
          what I understand. They're in the
          preamble stages. I know I can't
          touch the local Mob or the
          Russians, but after I collect the
          proper evidence maybe I can show
          them to the guys who can.---

We hear distorted talking through the other line...

                    DETECTIVE TRAVIS PARKER
          I don't know, CHIEF, but I'll work
          on getting more sources, more
          info. I haven't slept in over 36
          hours, and I gotta go home and see
          my family, get some rest, or I'll
          be no good to nobody. But, I
          assure you, boss, I'll get to the
          bottom of it.---

The sleepy-eyed DETECTIVE hangs up and places another
call...

                         DETECTIVE TRAVIS PARKER
                    (talking into the
                    phone,leaving a
                    voice-mail)
               --Hey, Honey, I know you're
               sleeping--I just want you to know
               I'm on my way home now. I can't
               wait to see you and TRAVELER.--I'm
               sure I'll see you before you check
               this message, however, I still
               gotta tell ya, you're the most
               beautiful woman in the world. I
               LOVE YOU, and my little TRAVELER.
               I'll be home ASAP.--
                    (hangs up the
                    phone)
               Thank You, Jesus, for my Family.

The DETECTIVE stops at a red-light. He looks around, no one
is in sight. The area is unusually empty; no noise, very
little-light.

Suddenly, a white-van pulls up beside DETECTIVE TRAVIS
PARKER...

He feels uneasy. His instincts are telling him something. He
loosens his holster as to make it easier to draw his pistol
if necessary.

                                        CUT TO:

EXT. CITY-STREET - CONTINUOUS

Fast as greased-lightning, 5 SHOOTERS jump out of the
white-van, armed-to-the-teeth; TOMMY-GUNS with 100-ROUND
DRUMS.

                         HENCHMAN #1
                    (preparing to fire)
               --Get 'Em, Boys...

                         DETECTIVE TRAVIS PARKER
                    (pulls his pistol
                    and fires)
               --No!!!

They shoot at DETECTIVE TRAVIS PARKER. He tries to evade, to
no avail; he gets hit multiple times.

His bullet-riddled car sways, and veers, but then stops. His
head rests on the steering-wheel, leaving the horn
blowing...No one is around, no one responds to the CHAOS...

                    HENCHMAN #2
          --Won't be hearing from him no
          more...

A MAN, dressed in a Surgeon's attire, with a unique white
ghost-like mask, which covers hit entire face and head, gets
out of the VAN.

The masked-MAN approaches the COP CAR.

TRAVIS PARKER is not yet lifeless, he's struggling to hang
on.

                    THE EUTHANIZER
               (speaks to PARKER
                through the
                shattered-window)
          --DETECTIVE. You don't look so
          good...this is what happens when
          you are nosey. When you know
          things you shouldn't. NOW--let me
          cut to the chase. Have you
          reported any of your findings, and
          if so who to? And, what else do
          you know?

                    DETECTIVE TRAVIS PARKER
               (laboring breath)
          --I haven't--told anyone anything.
          And--All I know is---YOU WILL NOT
          GET AWAY WITH ANY OF IT...

                    THE EUTHANIZER
          -You know, being on the
          verge-of-death, if I were you I
          wouldn't talk so much...ah,
          anyway. You have a good night,
          friendo.

                    DETECTIVE TRAVIS PARKER
          --I--Have--To---Know. Who are You?

THE EUTHANIZER pulls a syringe from his coat pocket, filled
with poison and potassium.

He quickly injects the defeated DETECTIVE...

                    THE EUTHANIZER
          --I AM THE EUTHANIZER, my good
          sir. Now, enjoy your rest, ha-ha--

DETECTIVE TRAVIS PARKER departs from life while hearing the
mad Doctor's laugh.

                                                    CUT TO:

INT. THE LAB CONTAINMENT CENTER - NIGHT

LM-275, LITTLE-BIT, all grown up, is in a cage, with myriad
other species of animals and many people of all walks of
life, also in confining cages.

He doesn't realize he's about to be transported to be
euthanized and dissected as his results have proven more
than successful; his senses are more advanced than MILSTEIN
ever dreamed...

LITTLE-BIT, or LM-275, is a perfect match for the
crossover-hybrid SUPER SOLDIERS that MILSTEIN has been
ordered to create by the COMINTURN.

                    THE DOG CATCHER
              (walks into the
              CONTAINMENT
              CENTER)
          --LM-275, your time is up, buddy.
          I'm here to take you to THE
          EUTHANIZER. You know the drill.

                    LM-275
              (growling)

Though grown-up now, LITTLE-BIT is still tiny.

The small dog perks up, and prepares himself.

THE DOG CATCHER detaches his key card from his vest.

He goes to swipe the ID-Reader, and it unlocks the cage. LM
pushes the cage-door open with all of his might, pushing
back THE DOG CATCHER, who falls on the floor.

LM-275 quick-as-lightning jumps down and grabs the ID-Card.

The one-eyed animal sprints with persistence toward the
entrance-door of THE CONTAINMENT CENTER. He, with the card
in his mouth, jumps up and, with success, swipes the card,
opening the door.

LM-275 escapes with ease; unseen.

All the other animals and people confined in the LAB go
nuts, reacting at the sight of the little-dog eloping...

                                                    CUT TO:

EXT. THE LABORATORY - MOMENTS LATER

LM-275 elopes through the ventilation-vent of the LAB. He
breaks it open and hops to the ground, about 25-feet. He's
like a cat, lands on his feet like it's nothing.

He dashes through the field that surrounds the LAB, alarms
sound, but with God's Blessing the little cycloptic-beast
manuvers through the field undetected and escapes with
simplicity.

                    LM-275
               (to himself,
                running with all
                he's got away
                from the LAB)
          --Now, I've got to find help.--

LM dashes into THE DARK WOODS surrounding THE LAB...

                                        CUT TO:

INT. THE LAB - LATER

THE EUTHANIZER wakes THE DOG CATCHER up from his unconscious
state...

                    DR. VLADIMIR MILSTEIN
          --What the hell happened?--YOU HAD
          ONE FUCKING JOB!!!---

                    THE DOG CATCHER
          --Boss, he--he got away, I
          couldn't stop 'em...FATE allowed
          it.--

DR. MILSTEIN slaps THE DOG CATCHER, back-handed...

                    DR. VLADIMIR MILSTEIN
               (slapping the dog
                catcher)
          --You Stupid Son-of-a---

                                        CUT TO:

EXT. THE DARK WOODS - LATER

In THE DARK WOODS, LM-275 discontinues sprinting. He finds a
light, a small glimmer in the night; he goes to it, and
stands under it, a light-pole out-of-nowhere.

He rests for some moments.

                        LM-275
                  (panting, tired)

A bird, A CROW, flies downward. LM thinks he's being
attacked; the dog falls back away from the blackish-flying
creature.

                        THE CROW
                  (lands on the
                   ground)
                --You could use some water, huh,
                young fellow?--

                        LM-275
                  (speaks)
                --Yeah, I really could.

THE CROW pecks LM-275...

Removing something...

                        LM-275
                --OUCH!!!--What the heck?

Destroys the device that was lodged in LM's skin...

                        THE CROW
                --Fret Not. I was merely removing
                and disposing of your RFID chip;
                so they can't track or find
                you...Now---There's a creek due
                west of here. You should be able
                to smell it, being that you can
                talk. Being that you're a
                successful experiment of THE
                LAB...they've made so many of us,
                haven't they? I managed to escape
                too, and like you, I was lost once
                I left the grounds. I didn't know
                what to do. I was so lost, I came
                back here till I was let go to
                AGENT ORANGE.

                        LM-275
                You know about THE LAB?

                        THE CROW
                --Yes, I know more than I let
                on...you--I've been following you
                since you left there. I came all
                the way from FLORIDA, to here, and
                        (MORE)

                    THE CROW (cont'd)
now I know why I came back...to
find you--to guide you. You're the
one that destiny has brought me
to. My Master--my Father--He was a
terrible man of many evil
deeds--his acts are too harsh to
speak of. He caged me for years, I
was a gift from DR. COTOMAN to
him; as they were in cahoots.
AGENT ORANGE massacred men, women,
anything that moved. I must redeem
myself from his onslaught, and I
know I can do so with you, LITTLE
one.--

                    LM-275
--You speak well for a bird.--

                    THE CROW
--That's the pot calling the
kettle black, huh?--

                    LM-275
--Where's the city?---I wasn't
expecting to wind up in THE WOODS
like this.

                    THE CROW
-You are exactly where you are
supposed to be, doing what you are
doing at this very given moment in
space and time.--

The CROW stretches his wings, and retracts them back in.
LM-275 is in awe of THE CROW.

                    LM-275
--How does it feel to fly? You
feel like Superman?

                    THE CROW
--To fly is to be free. My wings
though, they're
deteriorating...Flying is good,
but you will do greater things
than that.

                    LM-275
--You gonna train me???--

                    THE CROW
--No, I'm gonna teach you.--

                        LM-275
          --Teach me what?

                        THE CROW
          --The balance between POWER and
          SELFLESSNESS.--

                        LM-275
          --Hit me, bird.--

                        THE CROW
          -Okay.-
                (smacks the dog
                 upside the head
                 with his wing)

                        LM-275
                (pawing his face)
          --Hey, I meant tell me the balance
          of whatever-the-hell you were
          talking about! Not literally hit
          me!

                        THE CROW
          --Follow Me.--

                        LM-275
          --I can barely stand, I need
          water. Where are you going?--

                        THE CROW
          --WHAT IS THAT TO THEE?---

                                        CUT TO:

EXT. THE CREEK - LATER

LM-275 drinks water from THE CREEK. The water is the best
he's had in a very long time. He gulps it.

THE CROW watches the canine indulge. Finally LM ceases
drinking, and looks to THE CROW.

                        THE CROW
          --What is your story,
          LITTLE-one?--

                        LM-275
          --My name is--was LITTLE-BIT. At
          THE LAB they called me
          'LM-275'.---I been living in a
          cage in THE LAB for the last
          couple years...before that, I was
                        (MORE)

LM-275 (cont'd)
just a baby, living with my Mama:
KIMBA, and my Papa: SAMPSON, and
my Uncle: SCOOTER. But---we all
got taken by THE DOG CATCHER, he
took us to the EUTHANIZER...I lost
my family. All of 'em...

THE CROW
--Loss is inevitable.--It makes us
who we are to become. If we all
were immortal, we would lose our
purpose, don't you think? And,
yet, still, although you have lost
so much, YOU HAVE SO MUCH TO
GAIN.---Do you know God? Do you
know THE LORD JESUS CHRIST?--

LM-275
--My Mama and Papa taught me about
God--He created Heaven, Earth, all
things were made by Him.--JESUS,
HIS SON, is the WORD MADE FLESH,
He sacrificed Himself on the Cross
at Calvary. He defeated Sin and
Death, and He rose on the 3rd
Day.---

THE CROW
--Very Good.---Do you know WHAT
God is?--

LM-275
     (puzzled)
--What?--

THE CROW
--God is Love, LITTLE-one.--LOVE
IS POWER. The Power of Love must
overcome The Love of Power, and
there is no greater Love than
this; to lay down one's life for
one's friends.--

LM-275
--Wow. It all makes sense, bird.--

THE CROW
--That is the lesson. Now, I've
shown you the water, you've drank
it, now be as such.---THE CITY
NEEDS YOU.--Good-Bye,
LITTLE-one...

THE CROW slowly turns into smoke and vanishes with the wind.

                         LM-275
               --Wait, Bird!?--Where am I
               supposed to go?--

The Moon lights up THE DARK WOODS, showing LM-275 the
way...he follows THE LIGHT...

                                        CUT TO:

EXT. THE GRAVEYARD/DETECTIVE PARKER'S FUNERAL - DAY

TRAVELER, a young 12 year old Bi-Racial girl, stands with
her White 30 something-mother at their beloved
father/husband's funeral: DETECTIVE TRAVIS PARKER

He was a vet. A gun-salute is done for the fallen
soldier/officer.

                    TRAVIS' PARTNER
               (puts his hand on
                CANDICE's and
                TRAVERLER's
                shoulders)
               --TRAVIS was a great man, and a
               great partner. I'm sorry for your
               loss, if there's anything I can
               do, let me know.---

They're silent. TRAVIS' PARTNER walks off.

                    TRAVELER PARKER
               (looks up to her
                mother)
               --Is he in Heaven?

                    CANDICE PARKER
               --If he isn't, God will have to
               deal with me.--Don't worry,
               baby-girl. He is at rest.

Men lower the casket into the grave-patch.

Tears fall from TRAVELER's eyes, as does her mother's:
CANDICE

The tears hit the grass, and WE CUT TO:

3 DAYS LATER:

INT. SCIENCE-EXPO BUILDING - DAY

A crowd of many people, young, old alike are gathered, sitting in cushiony chairs.

They are sitting quietly, listening to DR. VLADIMIR MILSTEIN speaking a sermon, if you will.

                    DR. VLADIMIR MILSTEIN
               (mid-sentence)
          --The potentiality of such a thing
          is glorious in its own right.
          Cross-Species genetics is proving
          to be a path that could lead to
          cures of all diseases, ailments of
          all sorts. We could regenerate
          people, or more precisely, they
          could regenerate themselves. Where
          I want to start, is with--wait for
          it--DOGS...yes, I know it sounds
          crazy, but I think, if done
          properly, we could harness the
          senses of DOGS: hearing and smell,
          specifically, and we could embed
          those particular senses into
          humans, enhancing them.--We could
          find every strength in every
          species of life and cure every
          weakness within ourselves. This
          could lead to a world without
          weakness, without sickness. We
          could create perfect
          armies---PERFECT SOLDIERS, all
          with cross-species genetics.---
               (keeps speaking)

                    TRAVELER PARKER
               (sitting in the
               crowd)
          --This guy is off-his-rocker. By
          the time he gets done what he
          wants, he'll have people sniffing
          each other's asses.

                    CANDICE PARKER
               (grabs her child
               by the arm)
          TRAVELER DENISE PARKER. Don't you
          dare curse, especially in public.
          I've told you time-and-time again.

                    TRAVELER PARKER
                         (sighs)
          Yes, Ma'am.

                    CANDICE PARKER
          --I didn't mean to be so snappy
          with you, baby. How about we dodge
          this stuff and go grab a bite to
          eat?

                    TRAVELER PARKER
          That would be awesome. Let's do
          it.

CANDICE and TRAVELER leave the SCIENCE-EXPO.

The speaker, DR. VLADIMIR MILSTEIN, watches them exit as he
drones on.

                                   CUT TO:

INT. CANDICE'S CAR - MOMENTS LATER

CANDICE is driving her daughter in a 2008 TOYOTA CORROLA
through the CITY.

                    TRAVELER PARKER
          --I can't wait for Summer to end.
          I'm eager to get back to school...

                    CANDICE PARKER
          What would you like to eat, dear?

                    TRAVELER PARKER
          McDonalds, I guess.

The Young TRAVELER has sadness written on her face.

                    CANDICE PARKER
          What is it, TRAVELER? What's
          bothering you?

                    TRAVELER PARKER
                         (bold and to the
                          point)
          --I don't think DAD had a
          Heart-Attack...I think he was
          murdered, Mom.

                    CANDICE PARKER
                         (starts crying a
                          bit)
          --Please, don't talk about your
                         (MORE)

                        CANDICE PARKER (cont'd)
          Father right now...I just want to
          enjoy this day.

                        TRAVELER PARKER
          --But, Mom, just listen--

                        CANDICE PARKER
                (screams)
          --STOP IT NOW!!!

                        TRAVELER PARKER
                (teary-eyed)
          ...Okay...

                        CANDICE PARKER
          We'll just order a Pizza. I'm
          taking you home.

It gets more quiet than outer space in the car...

                        CANDICE PARKER
          Your---Your Dad---HE WAS GUNNED
          DOWN...now, please, I'm telling
          you so you know, but, don't bring
          it back up.--

                        TRAVELER PARKER
          --Who? Who killed him?

                        CANDICE PARKER
          --I don't know...please, baby,
          just leave it alone.

                        TRAVELER PARKER
          Yes, Ma'am.

                                        CUT TO:

EXT. CITY-STREET - MOMENTS LATER

CANDICE is at a light on an outer-road of the city...

She is at a red-light, much like her husband was that night.

Out-of-no-where two junkies appear from the blackness of the
shadows.

They break TRAVELER's window.

CANDICE tries to drive off, but one of the CARJACKERS
reaches in through the passenger side and grabs CANDICE, and

puts the car in park.

The second CARJACKER runs to the driver-side and attempts to open the door, however he's unsuccessful.

CANDICE and TRAVELER fight for their lives...

                    CANDICE PARKER
        LEAVE US ALONE!!!

                    TRAVELER PARKER
        Don't hurt my MOM!!!

Miraculously, a huge cinder-block comes crashing down and hits the CARJACKER that is on the driver's-side.

LM-275, within moments, appears in front of CANDICE's car.

He barks as loud and as strong as he can to warn the CARJACKERS.

They respond, and both tuck-tail.

LM-275 stands there, hoping that maybe the people he's helped will help him.

He starts toward the car.

As the CARJACKERS vanish, TRAVELER and CANDICE exit the vehicle and pick up LM-275.

                    TRAVELER PARKER
        He literally just saved us, Mom.
        He's gotta be a guardian angel or
        something.

                    CANDICE PARKER
        You don't even have to ask me,
        we're taking this Little Guy Home
        with us.

                    TRAVELER PARKER
        Thank You, Mom.

                    CANDICE PARKER
        You're welcome, sweetheart...let's
        get in the car and go home.

                                CUT TO:

INT. CANDICE'S CAR - CONTINUOUS

LM-275 melts in TRAVELER's arms, they've both found their
new best-friend and they know it, so does CANDICE.

                    CANDICE PARKER
          --I wonder what the other pets are
          going to think about this
          little-guy?--Oh, and you're
          bathing him when we get home. No
          dirty-dogs are sleeping in my
          house.

                    TRAVELER PARKER
          The others will love him. And,
          yes, I'm going to bathe him
          tomorrow morning. He smells like
          ass.

                    CANDICE PARKER
          -TRAVELER DENISE PARKER! Stop that
          cursing!

The young girl cracks a smile, so does her mom.

                    CANDICE PARKER
          I'm so distracted, I forgot to
          call the cops...but then again,
          what am I going to say? That we
          were being CARJACKED, and we were
          saved by a 13 pound dog?

                    TRAVELER PARKER
          --Sounds reasonable to me.

                                        CUT TO:

EXT. THE PARKER'S HOME - LATER

CANDICE parks her car, She, TRAVELER, holding LM-275 exit
the vehicle.

TRAVELER drops LM in the front yard to see if he has to use
the bathroom.

He is in awe of the property...

                    LM-275
               (to himself)
          --This is prime real-estate for
          peeing.---

The tiny-Goodfella cocks his leg several times in one-spot, and he does his thing.

TRAVELER laughs, because LM starts scraping the ground with his paws, causing her to be hit with grass right in the face.

>   TRAVELER PARKER
>   (to LM, picking
>   him up)
>   --C'mon, buddy, you need to meet
> your new friends.

CANDICE is quiet, and simply cracks a beautiful smile at her daughter and the dog.

They enter their HOME.

>   CUT TO:

INT. THE PARKER'S HOME - LATER

TRAVELER and CANDICE enter their home, they have multiple dogs already there; as well as a cat, named BART, and a fish named FLASH.

There's a "doggie-door" embedded in the HOME's Front-Door, it's closed; TRAVELER opens it, but the dogs remain, cautiously observing LM...

They're caught-off-guard by the entrance of LM-275. The dogs speak, pseudo-telepathically. They make grunts, and what not, communicating specific words to one-another.

>   TRAVELER PARKER
>   (to her mom)
>   --I wonder what this 'LM-275'
>   means on his collar, mom. What if
>   he's missing from somewhere?--
>
>   CANDICE PARKER
>   --He found us, we're keepin'
>   him.--
>
>
>   TRAVELER PARKER
>   (hugs LM-275
>   tightly)
>   --You hear that, buddy?
>   (contemplating)
>   --LM-275, you need a real name.--

                    LM-275
               (being held,
                talking to the
                other dogs)
          --You filthy mutts better not put
          a single paw on me or I'll---

                    TRAVELER PARKER
               (to her dogs)
          CADMUS, BRIDGET THE MIDGET, ZEUS
          THE MOOSE, meet your new family
          member!

TRAVELER drops LM-275 to the floor. TRAVELER and her mother
mess around in the kitchen, with a bird-eye view of the dogs
interactions. TRAVELER wants the dogs to socialize. They
just smile, knowing they won't harm one another. They have
their dogs trained, and LM, he knows better.

But, having just escaped from a experimental-lab, he's quite
anti-social.

                    CADMUS
          --I'm CADMUS, who you be,
          little-one?

CADMUS is a bull-mastiff. He's white, with brown spots,
floppy ears, muscular, and kind of dim-witted.

                    LM-275
          I'm just a dog tryna get by, dude.

                    ZEUS
          --I'm ZEUS. TRAVELER calls me
          'ZEUS THE MOOSE'.

ZEUS is a grey-blue pit-bull. Bulky, hulk-like, yet sweet,
and a bear at heart.

                    LM-275
               (to ZEUS, and
                CADMUS)
          -That's nice to know shit for
          brains. All brawn, you two, huh?
               (to BRIDGET)
          --And, who are you, sweetheart?

                    BRIDGET THE MIDGET
               (british accent)
          I'm BRIDGET. I'm a retired
          show-dog. And, no. I'm not giving
          you any of my "goodies". SO DON'T
          EVEN THINK ABOUT IT.

                     LM-275
--Why does she call you a MIDGET?

              BRIDGET THE MIDGET
--Because, I'm like a
little-human...and, because, she
loves me. She's my--OUR--TRAVELER.

BRIDGET THE MIDGET, as TRAVELER calls her, is a
French-poodle, but CANDICE got her from a British-Nanny who
was selling pups, one of which happened to be BRIDGET.

BRIDGET is gray and black, with "fur-boots", and a sort-of
Afro, her most distinctive feature.

LM sniffs BRIDGET down, as ZEUS and CADMUS react
apprehensively.

BART comes out of nowhere to meet the little showstopper,
LM-275. BART THE CAT is orange; a slim version of Garfield,
if you will.

                BART THE CAT
          (with a french
          accent)
--Wow, another primitive canine.
How shameful.

                    LM-275
          (walks up to and
          circles BART THE
          CAT)
--Who you callin' shameful,
mister?

                BART THE CAT
          (with an even more
          french accent)
--You, you little-shit! Now,
back-off, or I will back you off!

BART jumps on the counter, and sees about FLASH THE FISH.
The cat and the fish, ironically enough, are best buds.

                FLASH THE FISH
          (to BART)
This one, he's different.

                BART THE CAT
          (to The FISH)
How do you mean?

                    FLASH THE FISH
          He's been through the ringer, this
          one.

LITTLE-BIT walks up to BART and FLASH, in his fish-bowl.

                    LM-275
          You guys know that I can hear you
          right? Talk to me, don't talk
          around me, please, good sirs? Now,
          what do you guys have to eat
          around here? I haven't had a
          decent meal in 2 years.

TRAVELER walks up with food, a can of Pedigree, and some
water, cold as the arctic.

                    LM-275
                (sincerely praying)
          Thank you, Jesus.
                (devours the food)

The tiny dog eats and drinks as if it's his first and last
time...

                    TRAVELER PARKER
          Boy, you're gonna make a good dog
          for us. Now, it's time for bed.
          Say Goodnight to the others.

                    LM-275
          --Goodnight, you little-turds...

                    BRIDGET THE MIDGET
          --Did he just--

                    ZEUS
          --Yep.--

                    BRIDGET THE MIDGET
          And, then he.---

                    CADMUS
          --Sure did.--

LM stares the dogs down. He's not fixed, so he has that
"edge"...

                              CUT TO:

INT. TRAVELER'S ROOM - LATER

TRAVELER carries LM to her room.

LM is awed by what he sees.

The very same superheroes KIMBA would read to him as a pup
are on TRAVELER's walls...the kid, despite being a girl,
loves superheroes and comic-books.

LM jumps down, and runs to her pile of comic-books, he
quickly spots a Spider-Man comic-book and gestures to
TRAVELER.

                    TRAVELER PARKER
          --Of course I'll read to you. I
          knew you were smart, but not that
          smart for goodness' sake.

TRAVELER reads an issue of the web-slinger to LM-275 till
they both fall asleep, isolated from the other animals.

This is the first true snuggling LITTLE-BIT has had since
his family was taken from him. He's got a new family...he
just knows it.

LITTLE-BIT opens his one-eye, seeing TRAVELER, she says,
verbatim:

                                        CUT TO:

                    TRAVELER PARKER
          --Goodnight, My Little Man.

And, the name stuck from there.

                                        CUT TO:

INT. THE PARKER'S HOME - MORNING

LM-275 awakens to a Sun-lit room.

He slept very well.

He exits the room, and proceeds to the KITCHEN where
TRAVELER is.

                    TRAVELER PARKER
               (talking to LM)
          LITTLE-MAN! How are you this
          morning?--time for a bath.

CUT TO:

45 Minutes Later, Traveler has finished bathing LM.

He's drying off, no towel, already shaken.

The small dog wags his tail with glee.

> TRAVELER PARKER
> You did great, buddy. Get yourself
> some food and water, my good sir.

TRAVELER shows LITTLE-MAN to his breakfast. He stops over
it, looks to the left, then to the right...He then eats and
drinks, rather quickly.

> TRAVELER PARKER
> Go ahead--outside, the doggie
> door. The other dogs are out
> there, go play. Then, we're going
> to THE VET, to see BOB.---

LITTLE-MAN walks through the doggie-door, outside to the
scenic property.

CUT TO:

EXT. THE YARD - CONTINUOUS

LITTLE-MAN walks up to a few spots, cocks his leg, and
whizzes on the spots.

He then starts sniffing around. As he does, ZEUS and CADMUS
walk up on him.

LITTLE-MAN moves with swiftness, taking a karate-type
stance.

> ZEUS
> --You gonna pee on the spot, or
> admire it?--

> LITTLE-MAN
> --Both. What are you two fools up
> to?--Can't you see I'm doing my
> thing here?

ZEUS and CADMUS go to pee on the spots LM doused.

> CADMUS
> You're peeing on our spots, buddy.
> This is a problem.

LITTLE-MAN ignores the two, and pees on a couple more different spots.

                    ZEUS
               (bucking up)
          --You got some nerve, you
          little---

                    BRIDGET THE MIDGET
          --Leave him alone, ZEUS. You too,
          CADMUS. Let him be.

ZEUS and CADMUS back off then walk off at the request of BRIDGET.

LITTLE-MAN appreciates this beyond measure.

                    LITTLE-MAN
               (to BRIDGET)
          --THANK YOU.--

BRIDGET walks to a patch of grass and begins eating it.

                    LITTLE-MAN
          Why are you eatin' grass?

                    BRIDGET THE MIDGET
          --I'm trying to go 'vegan'. I love
          eating grass.

                    LITTLE-MAN
               (pees on another
                spot)
          --Vegan, huh? Good luck with that.

LITTLE-MAN scratches the ground, slinging grass in BRIDGET's face.

                    BRIDGET THE MIDGET
               (getting hit with
                grass)
          --C'mon, man, you're getting my
          coat all grassy!!!

LM stops and observes BRIDGET with her gray-and-black afro.

                    LITTLE-MAN
               (observing her
                afro)
          It just hit me, Bridget.--You look
          like Don King in '85.---

                    BRIDGET THE MIDGET
                    (puzzled)
            Who the heck is Don King?

                                        CUT TO:

EXT. THE VET - MORNING

LITTLE-MAN is getting checked up at THE VET, before
entering, TRAVELER and CANDICE allow him to pee in the grass
beside the building.

A WOMAN walks up spontaneously...

                    WOMAN
                (to TRAVELER, in
                reference to
                LITTLE-MAN)
            --Wow, He's got quite a
            package.--He's hung like an
            African Race Horse!---

                    CANDICE PARKER
            --Ma'am that is wholly
            inappropriate.---

The weirdo WOMAN walks away, understanding she overstepped a
boundary.

                    TRAVELER PARKER
                (to her mom)
            --They have race-horses in
            Africa???---

CANDICE PARKER rolls her eyes. After LITTLE-MAN pees, her
and TRAVELER enter THE VET with their newly acquired dog.

                                        CUT TO:

INT. THE VET - CONTINUOUS

LITTLE-MAN reluctant as is, becomes petrified by the way the
vet looks on the interior; it's not busy at all, no one is
there, except for a couple of barking dogs in the back
awaiting pick-up.

THE VET reminds LM of MILSTEIN's LAB, but he shakes it off,
he knows TRAVELER has his best interest at heart.

LITTLE-MAN meets BOB THE VET.

                    BOB THE VET
              (enters in from
               the back of the
               building)
     --Well, hello, ladies! Who is this
     furry fella you've brought today?

                  TRAVELER PARKER
              (holding LM-275)
     --BOB, this is my LITTLE-MAN.--

                  CANDICE PARKER
     --We just wanna get him his shots,
     all-and-all of 'em, if you would
     please, doc.

                    BOB THE VET
     --Sure, sure, how are you two on
     this day The Lord has made, huh?--

                  TRAVELER PARKER
              (petting
               LITTLE-MAN)
     --We're doing well, BOB.

                  CANDICE PARKER
     --Everything is starting to smooth
     out...We--We're still dealing with
     losing TRAVIS, but we're making
     it.

BOB walks up to TRAVELER and CANDICE, puts his hands on
their shoulders.

LITTLE-MAN realizes BOB is GOOD.

                    BOB THE VET
     --I'm sorry for your loss. You
     have my deepest sympathies.--It'll
     be okay, you two will pull
     through. And, hey, you have this
     guy as a new addition to the
     family.

CANDICE and TRAVELER smile at BOB, and they adoringly smile
at LM-275.

                    BOB THE VET
              (extends his arms
               out to grab LM)
     --Does he have records already?
     Where's he from?

> TRAVELER PARKER
> --We found him by--

> CANDICE PARKER
> (cuts TRAVELER off)
> --It's a long, drawn out story.
> We'll just--just start his records
> here, and give him all the
> necessaries, please.--

> BOB THE VET
> (holding LM-275)
> --You got it, CANDICE. His collar
> says: 'LM-275', what's that in
> reference to?--

TRAVELER and CANDICE just stand there blank, they don't know
what the tag means.

> TRAVELER PARKER
> --It's just--how we found 'em.

> BOB THE VET
> --I'll just put that on the sheet
> till you guys get a new collar for
> him. You know, just as a
> formality, I gotta put what's on
> his tag on the sheet; just in case
> something happens, I know the dog.
> So---
> (fills out the
> appt sheet)
> "LM-275" it is...okay, guys, give
> me 30 minutes, and I'll be done
> with him. Shots and all.

33 MINUTES LATER:

LITTLE-MAN is utterly petrified, but he keeps his composure.
When he sees TRAVELER and CANDICE he perks up, and shrugs
the fear right off.

> BOB THE VET
> --He did wonderfully. He's a good
> dog, I like this 'LITTLE-MAN'.

> CANDICE PARKER
> --Good, BOB. Good. How much do we
> owe ya'?

> BOB THE VET
> --No Charge, Miss Candice. It's
> the least I can do.

                    CANDICE PARKER
          --Well, thank you. That's very
          much appreciated.

BOB hands LITTLE-MAN to TRAVELER.

                    BOB THE VET
          --Miss Traveler, you take good
          care of this one. And, you,
          LITTLE-MAN, you take care of these
          two.--

                    TRAVELER PARKER
          --Yes, Sir.--

LITTLE-MAN, with his one-eye, winks at the good doctor.

                                        CUT TO:

EXT. CITY STREET - MOMENTS LATER

TRAVELER, holding LITTLE-MAN, walks with her Mom from the
VET's office to their car.

                    TRAVELER PARKER
          --I think BOB has a crush on you,
          MOM.--

                    CANDICE PARKER
          --I'll say.--You ready to go back
          to the house?

                    TRAVELER PARKER
          --No, me and LITTLE-MAN need 20
          bucks. We're gonna take the Subway
          through THE CITY. I'ma show him
          the works of New York.--

                    CANDICE PARKER
          --No, Ma'am. Not
          happening.--You're not going out
          in THE CITY alone.

                    TRAVELER PARKER
          --I won't be alone, I'll have
          LITTLE-MAN.

                    CANDICE PARKER
          --No!--

                    TRAVELER PARKER
          To hell with this.

TRAVELER snatches her Mother's purse, retrieves 20 dollars, and she and LITTLE-MAN take off running away from CANDICE.

> TRAVELER PARKER
> --C'mon LITTLE-MAN, to the Subway,
> buddy!!!

> CANDICE PARKER
> TRAVELER DENISE PARKER, You're in
> such Deep-Shit when you get
> home!!! You hear Me, Girl?!!!
> You're gonna be grounded for a
> Year!!!

>   CUT TO:

INT. THE SUBWAY - MOMENTS LATER

Out of breath, LITTLE MAN and TRAVELER sit on THE SUBWAY, awaiting transport.

> TRAVELER PARKER
> --LITTLE-MAN, you're gonna love
> this day. We're going places...by
> day's end, you'll have seen most
> all NYC.

LITTLE-MAN wags his tail, he sits across from TRAVELER.

No one bothers her or the dog.

They just ride...

>   CUT TO:

INT. STATUE OF LIBERTY - DAY

TRAVELER, holding LITTLE-MAN in her arms, takes the tiny dog up to the top floor of the STATUE OF LIBERTY.

She then confides in him.

> TRAVELER PARKER
> --This place, LITTLE-MAN, it gives
> me peace. FREEDOM IS EVERYTHING.
> This STATUE, it is the symbol for
> LIBERTY...for JUSTICE.==I'm just a
> kid, but I've figured out
> first-hand, that without FREEDOM,
> there can be no Prosperity, no
> success, for anyone. America is a
> place of liberty, and it must be
>   (MORE)

                    TRAVELER PARKER (cont'd)
          PROTECTED, by all those who can
          protect it. Men die every single
          day for this country. They die
          fighting for the idea of freedom,
          and to ignore that is treasonous.
          Rather, we as Americans, you're an
          AMERICAN too, LITTLE-MAN, we must
          PROTECT FREEDOM AT ALL COSTS...you
          know what I mean, buddy?==

With his one good-eye, LITTLE-MAN looks at HIS TRAVELER with
pure love, as he understands what she is saying entirely.

She and LITTLE-MAN, after viewing the STATUE OF LIBERTY,
leave it and go elsewhere.

                                             CUT TO:

EXT. TRUMP-TOWER - MOMENTS LATER

TRAVELER and LITTLE-MAN are right outside TRUMP-TOWER; a
colossal, shiny building...

They proceed to enter.

                                             CUT TO:

INT. TRUMP-TOWER - CONTINUOUS

TRAVELER is halted by a guard of THE TOWER.

LITTLE-MAN, without a leash stops too.

                    TRUMP TOWER GUARD
          --Little Miss, you can't bring
          that animal in here.

                    TRAVELER PARKER
          --He's my service-dog.

                    TRUMP TOWER GUARD
          --I'm going to have to ask you to
          leave. You and this mangy beast.--

LITTLE-MAN is offended by this rhetoric, as is TRAVELER.

LITTLE-MAN proceeds to poop on the TRUMP-TOWER floor,
defiling it, humorously. TRAVELER laughs.

                     TRAVELER PARKER
                  (to the guard)
          --Touch me, or my dog, and I'll
          sue. I'll own this place by next
          week.

                     TRUMP TOWER GUARD
          --You little---

                     TRAVELER PARKER
          --Did you know, sir, that all dogs
          shit facing 'TRUE NORTH'?--

                                        CUT TO:

EXT. TRUMP-TOWER - CONTINUOUS

TRAVELER and LITTLE-MAN scurry hurriedly out of TRUMP TOWER,
with the guard chasing them.

                                        CUT TO:

EXT. THE COMIC-BOOK STORE - MOMENTS LATER

TRAVELER, walking beside LITTLE-MAN, reaches her favorite
COMIC-BOOK STORE, in it is a "Secret Stash".

They proceed to enter.

                                        CUT TO:

INT. COMIC-BOOK STORE - CONTINUOUS

Entering, LITTLE-MAN, with HIS TRAVELER, sees the COMIC-BOOK
STORE INTERIOR and nearly faints. He's only read a handful
of comics, but this Store has thousands of all types and
varieties of SUPERHEROES.

LITTLE-MAN is in a state of pure-bliss. The workers know
TRAVELER, they don't even tell LM to leave.

                     COMIC BOOK MAN
          --Hey there, MISS TRAVELER! How
          are ya? Who's your buddy there?

                     TRAVELER PARKER
          --I'm doing good, sir. This is my
          dog: LITTLE-MAN. LITTLE-MAN, meet
          the COMIC-BOOK MAN.

                    COMIC BOOK MAN
--You two, you get a 50% discount,
on me. Pick out any comic you
like, MISS TRAVELER.---

                    TRAVELER PARKER
          (to COMIC BOOK MAN)
Yes, sir.
          (Looks down at
           LITTLE-MAN)

                    TRAVELER PARKER
          (talking to
           LITTLE-MAN)
--My UNCLE HIPPY-JOHN told me
about this place. He has a MUSTANG
to kill for. So, what do you
think? It's great, huh,
LITTLE-MAN? Pick out any 3 you
want, okay?

LITTLE-MAN goes to town searching...

The small dog picks out 3 COMICS at his eye-sight level on
the first row, for a very reasonable price, all
'SPIDER-MAN'...

                    COMIC BOOK MAN
--What? Does he read comics???

                    TRAVELER PARKER
--I read 'em to him, but he
understands 'em. Heck, he probably
does know how to read to be
honest. Smartest dog I've ever
encountered.---

                    COMIC BOOK MAN
          (to the dog)
--LITTLE-MAN, that name makes you
sound like you're a Superhero,
buddy, ha.
          (pets LM)
--Ya'll have a good evening,
TRAVELER. Thank you for your
business.

                    TRAVELER PARKER
--Yes, sir, you have a good
evening as well.==

                                        CUT TO:

TRAVELER, with 3 comics, picks LITTLE-MAN up, and they exit
THE COMIC BOOK STORE.

                                    CUT TO:

EXT. THE CITY STREET - MOMENTS LATER

LITTLE-MAN and TRAVELER are walking down the street.

TRAVELER sees THE ICE-CREAM man with his cart. She proceeds
to the cart, LITTLE-MAN follows right by her side.

                    ICE-CREAM MAN
          --Hello, little-miss! How are you
          and your furry friend today?!

                    TRAVELER PARKER
          --We're wonderful, sir, thank you.
          Can we have two vanilla-filled
          cones, please?

LITTLE-MAN suddenly feels unsettled. A type of
"Doggie-Sense" transpires in him, he can hear CHAOS
brewing...

                    ICE-CREAM MAN
          --Yes, Ma'am, indeed...you two, no
          charge.--It's on me.--

                    TRAVELER PARKER
                 (turning around)
          --Hear that, LITTLE-MAN?
          Free---Where the heck did he go?!

LITTLE-MAN has disappeared.

                    ICE-CREAM MAN
          --I didn't see him leave, miss.
          Maybe he walked around the corner
          or something.

                    TRAVELER PARKER
          --Hold the cones, sir. I gotta get
          my dog back, I'm gonna wait here
          for a few minutes, hopefully he'll
          come back. He couldn't have went
          too far.

TRAVELER is saddened by LITTLE-MAN's absence.

She waits patiently, optimistically; hoping he'll just
return to her.

                                              CUT TO:

EXT. BANK - AFTERNOON

4 Thugs, ROBBERS, prepare automatic weapons as they near the
entrance of a NYC BANK.

Two of the ROBBERS shoot the two GUARDS inside in the legs
from outside, and then the three men enter the BANK with
pure dominance over the people who see their only
protection, the GUARDS, flailing in their own blood.

                    GUARD 1
               (heard yelling in
                pain)
          Aah!!!

                    GUARD 2
               (passing out)
          --Holy--Holy Hell...
               (goes unconscious)

                                              CUT TO:

INT. BANK - CONTINUOUS

The 4 ROBBERS intimidate and harass the many customers and
employees. The guards are knocked out cold, they're in
shock...

                    BANK ROBBER #1
          --Any of you pricks move, and I'll
          put a bullet in all of ya!---

                    BANK ROBBER #3
          He'll do it folks!

                    BANK ROBBER #2
               (points his weapon
                at the head of
                the manager)
          --Give us all the loose-cash,
          asshole, no dye-packs, or you bite
          the dust!

BANK ROBBER 2 proceeds to escort the MANAGER to the door of
the primary safe.

As he does, the lights start flickering in the bank. It gets
extremely quiet...

                    BANK ROBBER #1
            What the hell is happening here!?
            Who pushed the button?!

Spontaneously, THE LITTLE-MAN jumps down into the bank,
through the ceiling.

The Dog hits BANK-ROBBER 1, and this scares the thief,
causing him to fire his weapon.

The burglar hits his own thieving friends; both of 'em,
literally.

Another bullet ricochets and hits BANK ROBBER 1 in the head.

None of the customers or employees have been hit or harmed.

                    LITTLE-MAN
                (walking out of
                 the bank)
            --Well, people, you need to hurry
            up and get an ambulance for your
            guys. Get the cops here too for
            the bad guys, then I suggest you
            all go about your business and
            have a blessed day.--

Almost everyone's jaw drops at the sight of the talking
LITTLE-MAN. One of the saved victims opens the door for the
tiny good-fella as he struts out.

                    CUSTOMER
            --Did we just get saved by a
            talking-dog?

                    MANAGER
            --Yeah, pretty much. I don't know
            whether to call the responders, or
            call a talent agent for that
            dog...

                                        CUT TO:

EXT. ICE-CREAM CART/CITY STREET - MOMENTS LATER

TRAVELER turns and finally LITTLE-MAN walks up, almost
smiling. TRAVELER is uplifted completely. She picks up
LITTLE-MAN.

                    TRAVELER PARKER
                (to LITTLE-MAN)
            --You little-shit, where were you?
            We're going home. Goodness
                    (MORE)

                    TRAVELER PARKER (cont'd)
     gracious you had me worried.

He just relaxes in TRAVELER's arms.

                    LITTLE-MAN
          (very happy)

                    TRAVELER PARKER
          (laughs a bit)
     --You--I can't even be upset at
     you.

                                   CUT TO:

INT. TAXI-CAB - LATER

A TAXI-CAB pulls up to the PARKER Residence...

                    TRAVELER PARKER
          (to the
           TAXI-DRIVER)
     --Thank You, MR. BICKLE.--It was a
     pleasure meeting you, good sir.
     How much do I owe ya?

                    MR. BICKLE/THE TAXI-DRIVER
     --No Charge. And the pleasure is
     all mine. You two be safe, okay?--

                    TRAVELER PARKER
     You got it.

TRAVELER and LM-275 exit the cab...she's holding the dog.

EXT. THE PARKER'S HOME - CONTINUOUS

The old Taxi-Driver rides off.

CANDICE runs from off the front-porch, and like a Lioness,
she snatches TRAVELER, the kid drops LM, and the MOM drags
the child in the house by the ear.

LITTLE-MAN follows the two into the HOME. The other dogs are
inside, awaiting to see what's the ruckus...

                    TRAVELER PARKER
          (being drug inside
           by her MOTHER)
     --Uh, Oh.--

                                              CUT TO:

INT. THE PARKER'S HOME - MOMENTS LATER

TRAVELER stands intimidated by her mother, who's in a
rare-mood.

LITTLE-MAN and the dogs go into the other end of the house.

                    TRAVELER PARKER
          -Mom, listen--

                    CANDICE PARKER
          --No, you listen, you will not
          leave this house, until I say you
          can. You will do work around this
          house to give me back my 20
          dollars which I know you stole and
          spent.--You Little-Miss, will have
          to earn your privilege of Freedom.
          Now, go to your room, I don't
          wanna see you for the remainder of
          the day.---

                    TRAVELER PARKER
               (holding back
                tears, holding
                her comics)
          --Yes, Ma'am.---
               (goes to her room,
                saddened)

                                              CUT TO:

INT. BACK OF THE HOUSE - CONTINUOUS

LITTLE-MAN is describing his exploits to the dogs, and BART
THE CAT. They're surrounding him, almost in a circle, as he
talks to them.

                    BRIDGET THE MIDGET
          --So, You--You stopped a Bank
          Robbery?

                    ZEUS
          --Ate Ice-Cream?--

                    CADMUS
          --And, You pooped in TRUMP
          TOWER?--

                    LITTLE-MAN
          --You better believe it.--The best
          day ever, this was.

                    ZEUS
          --Traveler must really like you,
          man.--

                    BRIDGET THE MIDGET
          We rarely get to go out in THE
          CITY.

                    LITTLE-MAN
          Take it from me, you guys need to
          get out more.

                    BART THE CAT
          Says the LAB Rat...

                    LITTLE-MAN
                 (to BART,
                  growling, angrily)
          --Excuse me? You Pussy!!! I could
          skin you alive!!!

LITTLE-MAN charges BART...

ZEUS and CADMUS hold him back, it takes both of them.

                    ZEUS
          --Calm down, LITTLE-MAN! He didn't
          mean nothing by it.

                    CADMUS
                 (restraining
                 LITTLE-MAN)
          --Don't let BART get to you, he's
          really a good Kat.

                    LITTLE-MAN
                 (relaxing)
          --Okay, you're right, guys. I'm
          calming down. I was overreacting.
          I just---

                    BART THE CAT
          --I'm sorry, LITTLE-MAN, I went
          too far.--

                        LITTLE-MAN
                  (melancholy)
            -I accept your apology, BART. It's
            all Good.--I'm gonna go check on
            TRAVELER now.--

                                        CUT TO:

INT. TRAVELER'S ROOM - MOMENTS LATER

LITTLE-MAN enters TRAVELER's ROOM.

The girl is praying...

She stops as he comes into the room.

                        TRAVELER PARKER
                  (wipes away her
                   tears)
            Hello, LITTLE-MAN, you startled
            me. I was just praying...

He walks up beside her and sits. She smiles.

                        TRAVELER PARKER
            --You know about Jesus,
            LITTLE-MAN?

He wags his tail.

                        TRAVELER PARKER
            He's the world's very first
            Super-Hero. Without JESUS, we'd be
            nothing, have nothing, know
            nothing.--Finish praying with me,
            buddy, then I'll read YOUR
            Comic-Books to you.

TRAVELER and LITTLE-MAN sit side-by-side, and the young
child prays as the dog eagerly listens.

                                        CUT TO:

INT. TRAVELER'S ROOM - LATER

TRAVELER and LITTLE-MAN are snoozing.

He awakens on top of his Comics...

The dog jumps off the bed, and proceeds to the living-room
area. He can hear the TV.

                                              CUT TO:

INT. THE LIVING-ROOM - CONTINUOUS

The Dogs, The Cat, CANDICE, even the Fish is asleep. The
News is on the television, LITTLE-MAN watches just in
time...

                         NEWS ANCHOR
                    (on the television)
               --Today, a terrifyingly shocking
               discovery was made...Over 200 dead
               dogs' corpses and nearly 50
               deceased people were found in a
               MASS-GRAVE in upstate...No
               connections have been made, the
               corpses are being removed from the
               site for autopsies and study, to
               see how and why this MASS-GRAVE
               was formed, and why those people
               and animals were in it. We will
               keep you updated.--

LITTLE-MAN, with his paw on the remote, turns the TV off.

                         LITTLE-MAN
                    (praying himself)
               --Lord Jesus, help me stop the bad
               men...

LITTLE-MAN, watching the other dogs sleep, lies his head on
his paws and goes out like a light.

                                              CUT TO:

INT. THE LIVING ROOM - MORNING

LITTLE-MAN wakes up at the sound of CANDICE and TRAVELER
fixing breakfast.

The other dogs are outside.

LITTLE-MAN awakens, however, to BART staring him in the
face, so close he's breathing on him; purring.

                         LITTLE-MAN
               --You sneaky son-of-a---

                       TRAVELER PARKER
               Good Morning, LITTLE-MAN!

The tiny dog gets up and gets moving.

TRAVELER pets him, and he stretches, drinks some water, nibbles some food; he has this determination about him as he exits the house through the doggie-door.

CUT TO:

EXT. THE YARD - CONTINUOUS

LITTLE-MAN, avoiding the other dogs, pees a couple of times, takes a quick dump. He then starts to leave the YARD.

BRIDGET, CADMUS, and ZEUS emerge in front of him before he leaves.

> BRIDGET THE MIDGET
> --Where the heck are you going,
> Mister?

> LITTLE-MAN
> The Subway, to catch a ride into
> THE CITY. I got work to do.

> ZEUS
> --You can't leave THE YARD.

> LITTLE-MAN
> (skirts past the
> dogs and sprints
> full speed)
> --Watch me.--

> CADMUS
> I kind of respect the Little-Guy.
> He's persistent.

LITTLE-MAN leaves the dogs, TRAVELER and the HOUSE.

CUT TO:

INT. THE SUBWAY - LATER

LITTLE-MAN rides the Subway. His doggie senses are leading him to the RUSSIAN MOB.

The SUBWAY stops, and LITTLE-MAN gets off. No one really even minds the little dog, on-or-off the transport.

CUT TO:

INT. BOB THE VET'S OFFICE - MORNING

BOB is doing paper-work, sitting at his desk.

BOB THE VET is a one-man show, he has no assistants, no help, and he does little-business, even being in NYC.

No one is there with him. They should be.

THE EUTHANIZER himself walks in, in full-Surgeon garb with his white-mask.

                    BOB THE VET
          --Can I help you, sir?--

                    DR. VLADIMIR MILSTEIN
               (locks the doors)
          I need a set of lungs, and
          eyeballs...yours will do.
               (lunges at BOB THE
                VET, and butchers
                him)

                    BOB THE VET
          --NO!!!

                                        CUT TO:

After doing his necessaries on BOB THE VET, DR. MILSTEIN cleans up the mess as if nothing ever even happened.

All the customers who've tried to come by see the closed sign, and have just gone elsewhere.

THE EUTHANIZER goes through BOB's paperwork. He sees the collar-name sheet, on it: LM-275

His LAB name on his collar is what BOB used to refer to LITTLE-MAN, innocently ignorant.

The address of TRAVELER and CANDICE is immediately found by MILSTEIN in the pile of BOB's papers.

                    DR. VLADIMIR MILSTEIN
               (in reference to
                LITTLE-MAN)
          --I've found you, you
          little-shit.--

THE EUTHANIZER exits BOB THE VET's office, having left the dead VET in the cooler in the back...in pieces...

                                        CUT TO:

INT. THE LAB - DAY

MILSTEIN, in his LAB, walks up to 4 highly secure cages, containing, SUPER-WOLVES...

He lets them out of their cages...they've been confined for a very long time. THE EUTHANIZER introduces the WOLVES to LM-275/LITTLE-MAN's scent with a few scientific items and tools he used only on LM.

The WOLVES salivate, growl, they're aggressive...

                    DR. VLADIMIR MILSTEIN
                 (to the WOLVES)
          --I UNLEASH YOU, go...FIND
          LM-275.--Don't stop till ya do...

DR. MILSTEIN opens the doors of the LAB, allowing the WOLVES to exit. They do, ravenous, roaring, in search of LITTLE-MAN...

                                        CUT TO:

INT. THE MEETING ROOM - DAY

BARNEY VERELLI, VLADIMIR RASPUTIN, and SALVATORE MANCINI: The three MOB BOSSES that control NYC, are meeting with DR. MILSTEIN/THE EUTHANIZER.

He stands, as the bosses sit and listen.

                    THE EUTHANIZER
                 (masked up)
          --We're on the verge, gentlemen.
          The verge of greatness. We will
          destroy this country, and we're
          starting here in THE BIG APPLE. My
          subservient has agreed to
          sacrifice himself. The ultimate
          sacrifice. We will attack soon.
          Very soon. The city
          leaders...their party will be
          crashed...and I have 'searchers'
          scouring for one of my subjects.
          Once I find him, RUSSIA, and all
          her soldiers, will be stronger
          than ever before.--This is what is
          going to happen--ANY OBJECTIONS???

BARNEY VERELLI and SALVATORE MANCINI shake their heads in disbelief and disagreement. They're the heads of the NY MOB. VLADIMIR RASPUTIN is the head of the RUSSIAN MOB.

RASPUTIN is, like MILSTEIN, a pawn of THE COMINTURN, so he
is in full compliance with THE EUTHANIZER.

                    SALVATORE MANCINI
          --You Communist piece of shit,
          this is my first of hearing this
          maniacal plan. What do you mean
          'THE CITY LEADERS'? You're gonna
          whack the Mayor? THE DA?--

                    THE EUTHANIZER
          --Yes.--

                    BARNEY VERELLI
               (concerned,
                somewhat scared)
          --This, we cannot allow. This is
          OUR CITY. Why would we do
          something so catastrophic? You're
          going too far.

                    THE EUTHANIZER
          --New York is already a
          catastrophe--although a
          magnificent one, it must be
          revolutionized,
          immediately.---CLEANSED, if you
          will.

                    BARNEY VERELLI
          --You Communists are insane.
          You're running around our country,
          infiltrating, and slowing
          destroying everything great about
          America. We're gangsters. Not
          terrorists.

                    SALVATORE MANCINI
          --You think you're a Supervillain,
          or something? You're a nobody, a
          RUSSIAN peasant who happened to
          become a scientist. All this
          terror you think you're about to
          cause, it ain't happening. I got
          100 shooters to stop ya, and they
          each have 100 themselves.

                    VLADIMIR RASPUTIN
          --Gentlemen, I wouldn't
          threaten---

                    THE EUTHANIZER
                (cuts off RASPUTIN)
        --OKAY. Well, now that all has
        been said and discussed, I will
        bid you fellas farewell. We will
        further discuss these matters
        sooner or later. No moves will be
        made until we can compromise,
        because you guys are the
        power-brokers, right?--LET'S JUST
        SHAKE on it, and call it a day for
        now, huh?

                    SALVATORE MANCINI
                (extends hand)
        --Don't do nothing you'll
        regret.--You try anything stupid,
        we'll have your head.

SALVATORE and BARNEY shake hands with THE EUTHANIZER/DR.
VLADIMIR MILSTEIN, and they proceed to the door.

However, as soon as they get to the door, before they can
open it, they collapse.

THE EUTHANIZER when he shook their hands, he gave them a
fatal shot of poison with a device attached to his wrist
that pricked them.

                    SALVATORE MANCINI
                (dying)
        --You--

                    BARNEY VERELLI
                (takes a last
                 breath)
        --Son-of-a-bitch.---

MILSTEIN just EUTHANIZED and murdered the MOBSTERS...

RASPUTIN is deeply disturbed, but still compliant with
MILSTEIN.

                    DR. VLADIMIR MILSTEIN
        --RASPUTIN, phone ALINKOV and
        CHEKOV. Tell 'em, we're going
        full-speed ahead. GOD SPEED...

                    VLADIMIR RASPUTIN
                (scared shitless)
        --Yes, DOCTOR.--

                                        CUT TO:

INT. THE MEETING-ROOM - LATER

VLADIMIR RASPUTIN is having a drink, in shock from the
powerful display of MILSTEIN...

He and his cohorts are smoking pot, snorting cocaine,
drinking, in bliss...

                    VLADIMIR RASPUTIN
                  (to his cronies)
          --I'm sick and fuckin' tired of
          that Doctor...he does nothing,
          he's a fuckin' virus among men...I
          hate that pri---

The Lights flicker...

A struggle can be heard as the light goes out completely.

Men grunting and yelling are heard, but no one can see.

Believe it or not, IT'S THE LITTLE-MAN, taking down THE
RUSSIAN MOB by Himself...

                                        CUT TO:

Suddenly the light returns, and RASPUTIN and his cronies are
restrained entirely...tied up; all by a little dog.

                                        CUT TO:

LITTLE-MAN takes one of the men's cell phones and dials
911...

                    911 OPERATOR
          --911, what is your emergency?---

                    LITTLE-MAN
          --Yes, I'm on 45th street; the
          luxury town-house, 803. I have
          with me the head of the Russian
          Mob, his people, and his
          drugs...please, send some guys to
          arrest these men. Thanks.

LITTLE-MAN hangs up. The men all look at him purely shocked
by his speaking.

                    LITTLE-MAN
                  (to RASPUTIN and
                   his guys)
          --Well, my job is done here,
          gentlemen. I bid you all farewell
                  (MORE)

LITTLE-MAN (cont'd)
in your jail-cells.

                                        CUT TO:

INT. 911 OPERATOR'S BASE - CONTINUOUS

The operator burst out laughing...

                911 OPERATOR
                (laughing)
        --Girl, you won't believe this.
        Some kid just called, said he has
        the Russian Mob leader in custody,
        and needs us to come take him and
        his men to jail. The cutest
        sounding kid...

                OPERATOR 2
        --Probly a prank.--

                911 OPERATOR
        Ima still send some guys over
        there. You know the rules. Gotta
        follow each call...

The 911 OPERATOR does her necessaries and gets a squadron
out to the call source location.

                                        CUT TO:

INT. MEETING-ROOM - MOMENTS LATER

LITTLE-MAN escapes unseen, as the authorities enter with
their guns drawn...cuffing the bad men, and confiscating all
their cash and dope.

                                        CUT TO:

EXT. THE YARD - CONTINUOUS

BRIDGET, by herself, walks through THE YARD, grazing as she
does.

She is observing beautiful mother-nature.

                BRIDGET THE MIDGET
        --What a gorgeous---

Something grabs her from the bushes, and takes her away.

                                              CUT TO:

ZEUS and CADMUS are outside now, they notice BRIDGET is
missing.

                    ZEUS
          LITTLE-MAN left, now BRIDGET is
          gone. Something is off. CADMUS, we
          gotta go, now.

                    CADMUS
          I feel it too, ZEUS. A bad
          feelin'. I smell--I smell WOLVES.
          Let's go find BRIDGET.

The two bulky dogs leave the property...

                                              CUT TO:

EXT. THE YARD - MOMENTS LATER

TRAVELER goes outside, seeing her animals have vanished.

                    TRAVELER PARKER
          --ZEUS THE MOOSE? BRIDGET THE
          MIDGET? CADMUS?---LITTLE-MAN???

                                              CUT TO:

INT. THE HOUSE - CONTINUOUS

TRAVELER storms into the house, panicking.

                    TRAVELER PARKER
               (distraught)
          --MOM, ALL THE DOGS ARE
          GONE!--Even LITTLE-MAN!

                    CANDICE PARKER
               (calmingly)
          --Don't worry. TRAVELER, don't do
          this right now. They're probably
          all together, they'll be back, I
          know it.--We have our errands to
          run, so let's get going. If
          they're not back by the time we
          get back, then we'll worry.--

                                              CUT TO:

INT. CITY-STREET - MOMENTS LATER

LITTLE-MAN is walking down a CITY-STREET, when suddenly, his
senses go haywire...

                    LITTLE-MAN
                 (struggling with
                  his senses)
            --BRIDGET is in CENTRAL
          PARK...WOLVES...Oh, no.---

                                        CUT TO:

EXT. CENTRAL-PARK - EVENING

The pack of ambushing wolves are holding BRIDGET captive.
She is unconscious.

They are standing over her, waiting for LITTLE-MAN.

The tiny dog arrives.

                    WOLF LEADER
                  (salivating)
            --You Little-Fool. You've fallen
          right into our trap. As you have
          come here to save your
          precious-poodle-girlfriend, THE
          EUTHANIZER himself and his
          squadron are in bound to take your
          sweet TRAVELER and her MOTHER...

                    LITTLE-MAN
          --Just let her go. That's all I
          ask. There's no need for this.

                    WOLF 2
          Do we look to be in a negotiating
          mood?

                    WOLF 3
                  (growls deeply)
          We've come to kill, nothing
          more...

                    WOLF 4
          You couldn't even take on one of
          us single-handedly...now you gonna
          take on all of us, LITTLE-MAN???

                        ZEUS
                   (appears with
                    CADMUS)
                --With our help!--

The 4 WOLVES surround LITTLE-MAN, CADMUS, and ZEUS...

However, the three DOGS are not afraid whatsoever.

                     WOLF LEADER
              --Let's tango, LM...

The WOLVES attack tenaciously. LITTLE-MAN like a dog-version
of Rocky, hits the leader with some quick, nasty bites and
scratches.

The leader grabs LITTLE-MAN and slams him to the ground,
standing over, he chomps at him.

ZEUS and CADMUS take on the other three WOLVES.

Two attack ZEUS, and the beastly dog holds them off and
fights them back.

CADMUS takes down WOLF 2 with three blows. The wolf is down
for the count.

CADMUS then goes to assist ZEUS.

                       CADMUS
              --ZEUS, I got this! You go help
              LITTLE-MAN!

ZEUS runs to aid LITTLE-MAN...However, LITTLE-MAN, somehow,
pushes the wolf-leader off of himself and head-butts the
wolf, disorienting the wild-animal.

                     LITTLE-MAN
                  (with power holds
                   the leader down)
              --You will surrender now! You will
              tell me everything! What is THE
              EUTHANIZER planning?!

The other WOLVES are incapacitated, and the leader is
defeated.

                     WOLF LEADER
              --I'm not talking, LM...

                     LITTLE-MAN
              CADMUS, you know how to neuter,
              right?

                    CADMUS
        --Yeah, we can take his right off
        of 'em, no sweat...

                    WOLF LEADER
                (wide-eyed)
        --OKAY! Wait! He's---He's gonna
        kill The Mayor at the CITY BALL. I
        don't know how, I just overheard
        them talking. He's taking your
        family, because he needs YOU.
        He--he keeps calling you "THE
        KEY"...

                    LITTLE-MAN
        --Where's he taking my family?!

                    ZEUS
        TELL US!!!

                    CADMUS
        --NOW!!!---

                    WOLF LEADER
        --He'll be at THE LAB. Where we
        all were---made---into what we
        are...

LITTLE-MAN paw-slaps the hell out of the WOLF-LEADER.

He, CADMUS, and ZEUS escort the unconscious BRIDGET away
from the WOLVES. She is still alive, just out-of-it.

They head through the park toward the SUBWAY...

                                        CUT TO:

INT. THE SUBWAY - MOMENTS LATER

ZEUS, CADMUS, and LITTLE-MAN and BRIDGET catch a ride on THE
SUBWAY.

ZEUS is carrying BRIDGET on his back.

She finally wakes up.

                    BRIDGET THE MIDGET
                (hops off of ZEUS'
                 back)
        --What in the heck? ZEUS? CADMUS?
        LITTLE-MAN? What happened?

                    LITTLE-MAN
          We had to save your ass, girlie.

                    ZEUS
          It's okay, sis. We took care of
          those Wolves. You're safe now.

                    CADMUS
          --We gotta hurry it up, guys. What
          if that bad man hurts TRAVELER and
          MAMA?

                    LITTLE-MAN
          He won't--I AM GOING TO STOP
          HIM.--You three go HOME, you'll be
          safe there. He's looking for me,
          not you. I'll go to him. THE CITY
          BALL is near here, I can't let the
          city leaders die.

                    ZEUS
          What are you gonna do?

THE SUBWAY comes to a stop. LITTLE-MAN prepares to exit.

                    LITTLE-MAN
          Just go home, I got this.

Two dopers sit on THE SUBWAY in utter awe, after hearing
LITTLE-MAN speak.

He turns to them before exiting.

                    LITTLE-MAN
                (to the two
                 tweakers)
          Don't do Drugs, guys.

                    TWEAKER 1
                (looks at his
                 buddy)
          We really gotta lay off the stuff,
          bro.

                    TWEAKER 2
          You ain't even lying, man...

He leaves the subway, and the doors begin to close. ZEUS,
CADMUS, and BRIDGET almost talk telepathically. Not,
LITTLE-MAN. He talks like a human.

                                        CUT TO:

EXT. THE PARKER'S HOME - LATER

A WHITE-VAN pulls up to THE PARKER's HOME, down the drive-way.

THE EUTHANIZER gets out behind 4 SHOOTERS.

They proceed toward the entrance of the HOME...

                                        CUT TO:

INT. THE PARKER'S HOME - CONTINUOUS

                    TRAVELER PARKER
                  (hurrying)
              -Mom, we gotta find our dogs.
            Where in the hell could they be???

Having brought in groceries, CANDICE and TRAVELER are stocking their KITCHEN.

CANDICE hears the VAN outside.

                    CANDICE PARKER
                  (looks out the
                   window)
              --Was that a car-door?---

Unaware of intruders at first, CANDICE and TRAVELER hear the commotion at the entrance of the house.

                    CANDICE PARKER
              --Oh, no.--

                    TRAVELER PARKER
                  (stirred up)
              --Mom? What do we do?--There are
              men in the house.

                    CANDICE PARKER
              --Go to your room, hide under your
              bed.--

                    TRAVELER PARKER
              --Yes, Ma'am.--

                                        CUT TO:

The SHOOTERS and DR. MILSTEIN make their way into THE KITCHEN after TRAVELER has hidden.

THE EUTHANIZER approaches CANDICE PARKER.

                    DR. VLADIMIR MILSTEIN
               (unmasked)
          --Hello, madam, am I
          disrupting?--You know, you have
          quite a beautiful home.
          Architecturally, it is brilliant,
          I mean so genuinely. Now---I
          assume your silence is from fear.
          Be not fearful of me, my dear. I
          simply must accommodate you and
          your sweet daughter to the realm
          of THE UNDERWORLD, as I did your
          husband...

                    CANDICE PARKER
          --YOU--you killed TRAVIS?---

                    DR. VLADIMIR MILSTEIN
          --Yes.--

THE EUTHANIZER is more than intimidating.

                    DR. VLADIMIR MILSTEIN
               (grabs CANDICE by
                the throat)
          --Come with me.==
               (to SHOOTERS)
          --GO INTO THE BEDROOM, GRAB THE
          LITTLE GIRL. ---

                              CUT TO:

INT. THE KITCHEN - MOMENTS LATER

One of the shooters is holding TRAVELER by the shoulders, in
place. Another has CANDICE held tight, as the EUTHANIZER
antagonizes them both.

BART THE CAT is out of the way, hidden. The other animals
are out saving BRIDGET. No one is there to help the PARKERS.

                    CANDICE PARKER
          --Why did you kill TRAVIS?--

                    TRAVELER PARKER
          --YOU!--You're the man, from The
          Science Expo! YOU KILLED MY
          DAD?!--

TRAVELER is fiercely angry...

                    DR. VLADIMIR MILSTEIN
          --Enough talk. You two are coming
          with me, LM-275 will meet me in
          due time, then I will finalize my
          work.---

                    TRAVELER PARKER
          --You killed my Dad...and now
          you're after my dog?--You
          mother---

TRAVELER breaks free from the SHOOTER, and strides to a
knife in the KITCHEN, she grabs it and goes to stab THE
EUTHANIZER.

However she fails, as MILSTEIN back-hands her across the
KITCHEN.

                    CANDICE PARKER
                (struggles,
                 strains to save
                 her daughter from
                 harm)
          --NO!! TRAVELER!!!

As a result of being hit so hard, the child falls into
FLASH's FISH BOWL, and knocks it onto the floor, breaking
it...

BART THE CAT emerges then-and-there, as FLASH is his best of
friends. He's a 'scaredy'-CAT, he knows he can't stop
MILSTEIN and the men with guns. But, he picks FLASH up,
quickly yet gently with his lips, no teeth.

He quickly eludes the SHOOTERS who jokingly take aim at the
innocent animal trying to save his pal.

                    TRAVELER PARKER
                (unconscious, on
                 the floor)

                    CANDICE PARKER
                (sobbing)
          --What have you done? YOU
          MONSTER!!!--

                    THE EUTHANIZER
          --It's not what I have done. It is
          what I am going to do that will
          truly shake the world.---

THE SHOOTERS and THE EUTHANIZER exit with TRAVELER and
CANDICE held in-possession.

                                        CUT TO:

INT. THE BATHROOM - MOMENTS LATER

BART THE CAT puts FLASH in the toilet, a source of water...

However, sadly, THE FISH, FLASH does not move. He died on
impact when knocked over.

Bart is traumatized by this loss. The whole family will be.

BART flushes FLASH.

                    BART THE CAT
                 (mournfully)
            -_God Bless FLASH THE FISH.--

                                        CUT TO:

INT. THE KITCHEN - LATER

BART THE CAT, deeply saddened, enters the kitchen. The dogs
are there now.

                    BRIDGET THE MIDGET
            --What the heck happened, BART?

                    BART THE CAT
            --The bad-man. He took TRAVELER
            and CANDICE. He--FLASH is dead,
            guys.

                    CADMUS
            --FLASH is gone? No. No. No. How
            are we just going to stand by? We
            can't just ignore this situation!
            LITTLE-MAN is going to stop these
            people? HOW? He needs our help!
            TRAVELER needs our help!

                    ZEUS
            --We're just house-animals. We'll
            get killed going with LITTLE-MAN;
            you heard those wolves. We're
            dealing with something beyond our
            selves, something only he must
            deal with. Besides, He has the
            Masterplan...

                    BRIDGET THE MIDGET
            --How do you figure?--

                         ZEUS
              -Because, he's THE LITTLE-MAN.--

                                        CUT TO:

INT. CITY-BALL - LATER

LITTLE-MAN makes his way into the building in which THE
ANNUAL CITY BALL is held.

THE MAYOR, DA, and other CITY LEADERS are present, enjoying
festivities, celebrating cheerfully.

Unbeknowest to them, the building is laced with explosives.

                    LITTLE-MAN
                 (walks on the
                  stage)

THE DOG CATCHER is present. He is dressed as a POLICE
OFFICER, and has a detonator.

                    THE DA
                 (drinking
                  champagne,
                  sitting at a
                  table)
              --Is that a fuckin' dog
              on-stage?--

                    THE MAYOR
                 (shocked)
              --It would appear so.--Hey,
              somebody get that dog off the
              stage!--

LITTLE-MAN with haste, pushes the mic to the ground, and he
speaks into it.

                    LITTLE-MAN
                 (trying to protect
                  the people)
              --Everyone, listen up! THERE ARE
              BOMBS THROUGHOUT THE BUILDING!
              Please, Evacuate now!

                    THE DA
              --Did that dog just talk?--

The people do not react, they laugh mostly; a talking dog,
you don't see that everyday.

However, LITTLE-MAN goes a step further. He pulls the
curtain back on the stage by-himself, before anyone can get
to him; revealing a set of gasoline-barrels full, with
explosive devices attached to all of them.

                    THE MAYOR
          --HOLY HELL!!! EVERYONE OUT!
          NOW!!!

The people panic, and all of them start to exit; except THE
DOG CATCHER.

Dressed as a cop, The Dog Catcher, stands up and confronts
LITTLE-MAN, detonator in-hand.

                    THE DOG CATCHER
          --You stupid mutt!--You think you
          can save these people? YOU
          COULDN'T SAVE YOUR OWN FAMILY!!!

LITTLE-MAN looks at THE DOG CATCHER, with his one-eye, and
he says these exact words:

                    LITTLE-MAN
          --I would rather die than make a
          butchery of my conscience. I
          FORGIVE YOU, but, you're evil.
          You're not harming another being
          ever again.

THE DOG CATCHER approaches LITTLE-MAN quite creepily.

                    THE DOG CATCHER
          --My orders are to blow up this
          building. I'm following through,
          and you're coming with me,
          LITTLE-BIT.--

THE DOG CATCHER pushes the button on the detonator. The
barrels and devices light up and count down from 10.

LITTLE-MAN evades the dog catcher successfully, and runs
between his legs.

The dog and the last of the civilians and leaders make it
out. THE DOG CATCHER stays behind, suicidal.

                    THE DOG CATCHER
          --Repentance, what's it good
          for?--

                                        CUT TO:

EXT. CITY BALL BUILDING/ACROSS THE STREET - MOMENTS LATER

LITTLE-MAN manages to herd some of the civilians away from the building prior to its explosion. None perish.

The CITY-BALL BUILDING goes up in flames as it blows up, with the dog catcher inside.

LITTLE-MAN in a rush, leaves the scene of CHAOS; to see THE EUTHANIZER.

He knows where he'll be: THE LAB

                         CIVILIAN 1
              --That dog...he--SAVED US.

                         CIVILIAN 2
                    (in awe of the
                     situation)
              --What in the hell just
              happened?--

                                        CUT TO:

INT. ROOM 777 - MOMENTS LATER

In ROOM 777 of the lab, VLADIMIR MILSTEIN, THE EUTHANIZER himself, has CANDICE and TRAVELER tied, bound, and gagged with a gun pointed at CANDICE's head.

The twos heads are close together. The intention of MILSTEIN is one-shot, two-kills...

The LAB is empty, no one is present. MILSTEIN has waited to take LITTLE-MAN's life, and he wants to do it alone.

                                        CUT TO:

THE LITTLE-MAN enters ROOM 777 as the door was cracked a bit. He enters cautiously, yet bravely, to confront the man that took his family as a pup and is trying to do so again...

                         TRAVELER PARKER
                    (distorted due to
                     rag in mouth)
              Mmm!!!---

                         CANDICE PARKER
                    (yelling through
                     rag)
              MMM!!!

                    THE EUTHANIZER
     --Hello, my furry little-friend!
     How nice of you to join us.
     Please, come closer. I knew you'd
     be here...FATE ALWAYS DELIVERS.

                    LITTLE-MAN
                 (struggles to
                  speak, but does
                  so)
     --Y-y-you don't have to do this.
     You can release my family, now.
     Or, Doctor, I will put you down.

TRAVELER and CANDICE are utterly shocked by LITTLE-MAN's
ability to enunciate words...

DR. MILSTEIN is even more surprised.

                    DR. VLADIMIR MILSTEIN
     You see, you can even talk now.
     You're evolving beyond my wildest
     dreams. Your powers are growing
     exponentially, and they must be
     dissected and applied! I've done
     the work I was meant to do. Create
     you...I've killed people, many.
     I've killed 274 dogs just to get
     to you LM-275. You are THE KEY to
     unlocking humanities' true
     potential. You single-handedly
     took down RASPUTIN--I'm not even
     mad--that's amazing--Your
     Power---Once I extract your gifts,
     I'll apply them to every soldier
     in mother Russia and we will storm
     the gates of Mount Olympus...---

                    LITTLE-MAN
     WHY?--

                    DR. VLADIMIR MILSTEIN
     --WHY NOT?---

                    LITTLE-MAN
     Because what's wrong is wrong.

                    DR. VLADIMIR MILSTEIN
     Okay, cut out the macho-hero
     bullshit, you stupid mutt. I'm
     telling you right now, all I want
     is your corpse. Trade yourself for
     these two, or I'm killing all
     you!!!---
                    (MORE)

                    DR. VLADIMIR MILSTEIN (cont'd)
               (presses gun to
               CANDICE's temple)
          Now, CHOOSE!!!

                    LITTLE-MAN
          No!

                    DR. VLADIMIR MILSTEIN
          So be it...

He turns the gun to LITTLE-MAN, and opens fire...

                    LITTLE-MAN
               (yelps)
          Ah!

MILSTEIN has shot LITTLE-MAN in the face, taking out his
other eye with ease.

The Dog struggles for a moment after losing his other eye,
but he persists through the pain and gathers himself.

                    THE EUTHANIZER
          --LM-275, you stopped my plans at
          the CITY BALL---So it's only fair
          that I at least get a little
          killing done tonight. It's reflex,
          buddy.

                    LITTLE-MAN
               (springs forward)
          MY NAME IS LITTLE-MAN!!! And--I
          CAN STILL SEE YOU!

The tiny dog jumps high, ascending, he presses downward on
the tool-filled metallic-table, flipping it...

Many of the tools fly directly toward MILSTEIN, he dodges
all except three syringes, filled with euthanasia, which
stab him in the torso and chest area exposing him to small
amounts.

The old-man goes down, and the weapon falls out of his hand.
He passes out cold.

LITTLE-MAN immediately, with great haste, approaches CANDICE
and TRAVELER, and with his teeth he unties them. They then
free themselves of their gags and blind-folds, and attend to
LITTLE-MAN, who has passed out from his gun-shot wound.

                    TRAVELER PARKER
          --NO! LITTLE-MAN! Please, don't
          leave me!

                    CANDICE PARKER
              (crying, picks up
               the dog)
          LITTLE-MAN, we're going to get you
          some help! You're going to be
          okay. You've saved us, now we're
          gonna save you!

The three exit MILSTEIN's shadowy LABORATORY safely;
MILSTEIN stays down...

                                   CUT TO:

2 WEEKS LATER:

INT. THE PARKER'S HOME - MORNING

TRAVELER awakens from her peaceful sleep. Her talking-dog is
lying on a palette of blankets in the floor, snuggled up,
grumpily snoring a bit.

The kid urgently checks on LITTLE-MAN, who has gauze, and a
wrap around his face, as well as a cone around his neck
surrounding his head---for his healing gunshot wound.

                    TRAVELER PARKER
              (runs up to her
               dog)
          Good-morning, LITTLE-MAN, are you
          okay?

                    LITTLE-MAN
              (rising from his
               slumber)
          --I'm okay. Could you grab me some
          more food and fresh water, please?

                    TRAVELER PARKER
          You got it, sweet-boy.

TRAVELER exits the room and proceeds to the kitchen...

After TRAVELER exits, ZEUS, CADMUS, BRIDGET, and BART enter
TRAVELER's ROOM---in awe of the mighty LITTLE-MAN...

                    BRIDGET THE MIDGET
          --LITTLE-MAN?--

LITTLE-MAN remains quiet.

                    ZEUS
--We just--we just wanted to---

                    BART THE CAT
THANK YOU.

                    CADMUS
--You saved our family. YOU ARE
OUR FAMILY. We gotta new fish,
too.

                    LITTLE-MAN
--You're welcome, ya turds...

                    BRIDGET THE MIDGET
               (stays back as
                ZEUS and CADMUS
                exit)
--LITTLE-MAN, you can have my
'goodies' anytime...you're MY
HERO...
               (leaves the ROOM
                with the others)

LITTLE-MAN waits for the dogs to move through to the other
end of the house with TRAVELER and CANDICE.

He then, speedily, removes his cone, wrap and gauze; the dog
grabs a black scarf that is out in TRAVELER's room and exits
through the window, leaving the property.

                                        CUT TO:

                    TRAVELER PARKER
               (walks back in the
                room with food
                and water)
--I got you some--

The little-girl sees that THE LITTLE-MAN has vanished...

                    TRAVELER PARKER
               (drops the food
                and water)
SHIT. Not Again...

                                        CUT TO:

EXT. NYC ROOF-TOP - LATER

LITTLE-MAN, as short as he is, still stands tall on an NYC
ROOF-TOP, ready to save anybody who needs saving.

He has TRAVELER's black-scarf wrapped around his face,
covering his blindness.

                    NEWS ANCHOR
                 (voice)
          The City was saved from ORGANIZED
          CHAOS, folks--The Russian
          mad-scientist, DOCTOR VLADIMIR
          MILSTEIN, who many are starting to
          call "THE EUTHANIZER", was
          arrested and has been charged and
          convicted with mass-murder,
          conspiracy to murder, illegal
          experimentation, among other
          heinous criminal acts; all of
          which he's admitted and plead
          guilty to. MILSTEIN has committed
          murder of animals and people on a
          mass-scale--He's admitted to
          having DETECTIVE TRAVIS PARKER
          killed.--He experimented on many
          people and animals for reasons
          unknown to us.--MILSTEIN even
          tried to kill the Mayor and many
          other city-leaders at the ANNUAL
          CITY BALL only to be foiled by a
          Shih-Tzu---The stories are true,
          people. There's a Dog in this
          City, who is watching out for
          us--He stopped the EUTHANIZER and
          his cohorts. That Dog is--

                    LITTLE-MAN
                 (looking over the
                 CITY)
          --If there's trouble, I'll find
          it. If there's a problem, I'll fix
          it. If a person needs me, I'll be
          there. If the city needs me, I'll
          save it. WHO AM I? I AM---THE
          LITTLE-MAN--

LITTLE-MAN has lost his sight, but not his purpose.

The blind Dog jumps from the ROOF-TOP, with no fear,
prepared to do work.

He can see better than ever-before, as his senses are even

more enhanced.

THE CITY needs him, and he needs it.

LITTLE-MAN, the tiny-Dog with a mighty-Heart.

                              CUT TO BLACK:

ACT II. THE CHIROPRACTOR DR. VEGAS

                              FADE IN:

EXT. THE LAKE-SHORE - MORNING

                              LOCATION: SOMEWHERE
                              IN FLORIDA - BRODY'S
                              ESTATE

                              YEAR: 1991

A 30-something White-MAN, a father, is fishing with his
young bi-racial(Black and White) sons, ages 4 and 6,
respectively. The MAN is BRODY BARNES, the boys, TECHNO and
KILO sit to his left and right.

The LAKE-SHORE is scenic, gorgeous. The grains of Floridian
sand are fine, the sun-light shimmers off each one
vibrantly. The trees sway with the wind, bending, flexing,
yet it's a more than pleasant day.

The three each have bamboo-poles, awaiting their next
catches.

                    BRODY BARNES
          --Evil comes at leisure like the
          disease. Good comes in a hurry
          like the doctor. Be prepared for
          both. If you boys are patient, the
          world will be in both of your'
          hands. All good things require
          time, like fishing...you're not
          trying to rush the fish into the
          bait. You're letting the fish
          itself fall for the bait.
          Men--they're like fish. Fallible,
          frail, slimy, being led to the
          slaughter; serving a greater
          purpose.--

                    YOUNG TECHNO
          --Men don't eat men, right, pop?

BRODY BARNES
--Men do only what they must to
survive, boy. You, me, and KILO
here, we thrive; we are above
these inadequate beings called
"men". I fought for our survival,
and now we will know nothing but
prosperity. Don't ever think for
one second that life is
guaranteed, however, because the
moment one basks in his confidence
and surety, he will be broken. The
Chaos Can Consume Anyone.--

YOUNG KILO
--What is Chaos?--

BRODY BARNES
--Power, my boy. CHAOS IS POWER,
if ORGANIZED appropriately;
FAIRLY.--Chaos is all around us,
yet it is calculated, precise,
structured. We need Chaos, but
without organization, it would
consume us, without question...

YOUNG TECHNO
Chaos is power. Power is good?

BRODY BARNES
Power is Everything, my sons.
There are two types of people in
this world: Those with Power, and
those Without. Now, both of you,
with your own free-will, must
decide which of those you will
become...I can implement as many
resources to ensure your success,
but only you two, yourselves, can
solidify your survival. As much as
I love the both of you, even I
can't stop you from succumbing to
CHAOS. Your mother--she---she was
too weak-minded to see that the
only way to live in this world is
not only with power, but with
ULTIMATE POWER. She saw me as
deranged. I have to instill in you
the drive, the desire, the will to
carry on MY LEGACY.

YOUNG KILO
--Where is Mama?--

                    BRODY BARNES
          --She's asleep, son. With the
          fishes...

                    YOUNG TECHNO
          --You killed her, didn't you?--

                    BRODY BARNES
                (tugs on his
                 fishing pole)
          --No...THE CHAOS DID...

BRODY seizes a huge Bass from THE LAKE-SHORE.

He grabs it immediately after taking it from the water, he
unhooks it, throws it in his cooler.

                    BRODY BARNES
          --Now, boys, let's clean our food,
          fry 'em and we'll feast like the
          Kings that we are.--

                    YOUNG KILO
                (refusing to stop
                 fishing)
          --Hey, I'm not done, pop.

                    YOUNG TECHNO
          --We wanna catch a couple more
          with you.--

                    BRODY BARNES
          --We can go to the shed and start
          preparing the fish or I'm throwing
          all of 'em back, then I'll beat
          the living-hell out of both of
          you. NEVER QUESTION ME AGAIN,
          either of you. I mean it, here and
          now.

"YES, SIR!" The boys say in harmony, with urgency.

Both the youngins remove their fishing lines from the water,
and gather their poles in a hurry to take home.

They run toward the shed beside the house, as BRODY carries
his bamboo-pole and the cooler.

He smiles at his boys.

TECHNO, the 4 year old, trips and falls...

                                        CUT TO BLACK:

FADE IN:

YEAR: 2018

LOCATION: LAS VEGAS

LAS VEGAS is a noisy place.

The City is alive, depraved.

Gamblers, Mobsters, No-Goods all over.

They fill the slot-machines with their limited money, and lose themselves in the process.

CUT TO:

INT. THE ROOM OF SCREENS - NIGHT

A MAN, in his early-30's, slight-build, light-skinned, dread-locks, sits at his office desk in his ROOM OF SCREENS...

This ROOM is filled with monitors all throughout, they cover the 4 walls, displaying various clips of films, newscasts...INFORMATION.

The man's name is TECHNO BARNES aka: TECH THE TYRANT. Crime pays for him; you name it, he'll do it, if it's lucrative or advances his technological inventory.

He sits calmly, patiently, cyphering through as much as he can with his red-robotic eyes. He had his eyes removed himself, and replaced with optical-cybernetics that allow him to scan things and gather information, much like a terminator...

He scrolls on the mouse of his primary CPU monitor with his cold-metallic fingers...TECH has cybernetic arms.

He lost his real upper-limbs at the hands of his own father, BRODY, after screwing up.

TECH had surgery to have his arms replaced with metal from the shoulder-down; his arms are fully functional, and they give him super-strength, among other features.

TECH has a top-tier IQ of above 160, and he's also one of the smartest street-thugs in all of AMERIKA.

His BODYGUARD walks into THE ROOM OF SCREENS, nearly out-of-breath somewhat on-the-edge.

                    TECH THE TYRANT
          --What's going on? Why so
          panicked?--

                    THE BODYGUARD
          --Y-your BROTHER is dead.--I--

                    TECH THE TYRANT
          --BY WHOSE HAND?!--

                    THE BODYGUARD
          --I thought it was retaliation for
          him killing THE ORDER BOSSES, but
          it ain't.---A Crack-Head.--JAKOB
          JUSTICE--out of NEW ORLEANS, is
          who killed your brother. The
          motherfucker took out KILO and all
          of his men; his whole operation,
          TECH...it's gone, man.

                    TECH THE TYRANT
          Leave me...now...

                    THE BODYGUARD
                (proceeds to exit
                 from THE ROOM OF
                 SCREENS)
          --Yes, Sir.--

A single lonely tear falls from TECH THE TYRANT's machine
eye.

                    TECH THE TYRANT
                (to his A.I)
          KARMA?

                    KARMA THE A.I
          Yes, Boss?

KARMA is an advanced operating system.

She is a type of A.I, yet unformed to a degree, primordial.

However, she assists TECH magnificently and with great
efficiency.

TECH, with vampire-like fangs, is eating his supper as he
scans the screens...he's eating HUMAN BRAINS with a side of
smoked EYES, drinking O-Positive Blood from a HUMAN SKULL.
He is OUT THERE...

                    TECH THE TYRANT
              (chomping, sipping
               from his
               skull-goblet)
          --Show me the feed of my brother
          getting killed--I must see how.

                    KARMA THE A.I
          Gathering now.

All the screens morph into a giant single picture. KARMA
shows the footage to TECH.

TECH sees: The crack-head, JAKOB JUSTICE, after escaping
with a gun in-hand, shoots ether-barrels outside of KILO
BARNES' BASE.

The flames engulf KILO and crew with swiftness. TECH is
utterly shocked.

                    TECH THE TYRANT
          --Okay, turn that shit off...where
          is this JAKOB JUSTICE?

                    KARMA THE A.I
          --He's been INVOLUNTARILY
          COMMITTED to a hospital:
          'LIFE-CONTROL'.--

                    TECH THE TYRANT
          --Ah, fuck that crack-head
          son-of-a-cunt. It's KILO's own
          damn fault he got killed. How the
          fuck are we gonna maintain our
          POWER without him though? Without
          THE ORDER? Fuck. KARMA, power
          down. I'll be back after-while.--

                    KARMA THE A.I
              (shutting down)
          Yes, Boss.

TECH discontinues dining.

He gulps the remainder of the blood from the Skull-Goblet.
TECH turns the skull upright, a little blood drips from it.
THE TYRANT speaks to the skull, it is the skull of BRODY
BARNES...

93

                    TECH THE TYRANT
                  (to the skull of
                   his dad)
          --SEE, FATHER? I TOLD YOU KILO
          WOULDN'T LAST...

TECH puts the skull down, grabs his gun, and exits his ROOM
OF SCREENS.

                                        CUT TO:

INT. MANSION HALLWAY - CONTINUOUS

TECH THE TYRANT, leaving his room of screens, struts down
his mansion-hallway, with black-and-white checkered
flooring.

There are statues throughout the hallway as well as
paintings on the walls.

                    TECH THE TYRANT
                  (narrating)
          ==WHAT HAPPENS IN VEGAS, STAYS IN
          VEGAS...I am Sorrow's Child. I'm a
          Futurist...I've seen the future.
          The fire, the ashes, the
          apocalypse. Something is coming,
          and it's only a matter of time
          before the game is up. Vegas is a
          place where life is literally a
          gamble.--Truth be told, I'm only
          out for my own betterment, as well
          as the expansion of MY OPERATION.
          I know my limits, and I exceed
          them daily. I'm not a kingpin like
          my father. I'm a pure criminal;
          most of my enterprise is
          illegitimate, which I don't mind,
          because I compensate for that with
          my underground fight club. I
          entertain the people, and I make
          out like a bandit; I just leave it
          to the show-runners, I don't show
          my face. No one can connect me
          alone, it's a communal experience
          for the fans and the fighters.
          People pay big to see my fighters.
          My father...I think he would be
          proud of what I've accomplished.
          It's strange, now, knowing that
          death has overtaken my older
          brother. He should've seen it
          comin'. I know my death is near
                  (MORE)

                    TECH THE TYRANT (cont'd)
          too, and I'll do whatever I must
          to stop it.---The only way to stop
          death, is with ultimate power,
          which I will accumulate by any
          means necessary. There's nothing
          stable in this world; CHAOS is my
          only music.==

TECH THE TYRANT EXITS HIS MANSION

                              CUT TO:

INT. TORTURE-CHAMBER - LATER

TECH THE TYRANT is standing at the edge of a metal-table in
a TORTURE-CHAMBER, smoking a fat joint.

Across from him is a MAN, tied down and bound, with
duck-tape around the mouth. The man is strapped to an
advanced slab.

The MAN that is being victimized is a CASINO OWNER: VALTORE
TOTINO.

TECH walks from behind the table and speaks, with his
deep-voice to the CASINO OWNER.

                    VALTORE TOTINO (CASINO OWNER)
               (fighting to break
                free)
          --Mmm!!! Mmm!!!

                    TECH THE TYRANT
               (puts out his
                joint by stomping
                it)
          --You know, this TORTURE-CHAMBER
          was owned by my Father, BRODY. He
          rarely even used it. He had a
          fascination with the idea of
          torturing people, hell he's gotta
          few hid across the country. He
          brought me to one a couple years
          before his passing--had my arms
          amputated while I was paralyzed,
          but awake.--Ironically enough, I
          like using these chambers; they're
          discreet and proficient. I can
          extract my food in peace from you
          wretched depraved fucks, and cause
          as much pain as humanly possible.
          I'll tell ya, VALTORE. I'm going
                    (MORE)

                    TECH THE TYRANT (cont'd)
to digest you, I'm going to take
your eyes, your Brain, and I'm
going to eat 'em. How does that
sound???
          (rips the tape off
           the man's face)
--I can't understand you with all
the tape, what was that?

                    VALTORE TOTINO (CASINO OWNER)
--You goddamn Psycho!!! Do you
have any idea what the fuck you're
getting yourself into? You have no
idea who you're fucking with!!!
You'll be dead by sun-up when my
guys find you!!!

                    TECH THE TYRANT
          (smiles with charm)
--My friend, GHENGHIS KHAN killed
over ONE MILLION MEN in ONE-HOUR,
all by equipping his armies with
the bow-and-arrow. Did you know
that DRAKULA was real? Yes, yes,
he was. Vlad the Impaler of
WALACHIA. He was a Prince, a
Christian in fact. Yet, he was so
fierce a warrior that he had
hordes of his enemies and
opposition IMPALED on the tallest
of spikes. He would then drink
their blood while his people
watched in awe. I will have that
type of power very soon, and I
only have to kill you and the
other 6 CASINO OWNERS to do it;
I'm going to drink all ya's blood,
and I'm going to takeover LAS
VEGAS in one fell swoop; tonight
you're signing over your casino to
me. I will own all the 7 major
casinos in LAS VEGAS by tomorrow
afternoon. MARK MY WORDS. I just
need to know the next meeting of
the bosses, and I may consider
letting you die a half-way decent
death.--

TOTINO spits at TECH unwisely...

                    TECH THE TYRANT
          --Bad Move. I'll find the meeting,
          I promise. And, the other bosses
          will die and give me their
          CASINOS, just like you. I don't
          need your signature for
          transference of ownership,
          necessarily...I can forge it...I
          honestly just need you out of the
          way. I need you Dead.--

TECH pulls a knife, and he slices VALTORE's abdomen open,
and the man's guts literally spill out of his belly...

                    VALTORE TOTINO (CASINO OWNER)
               (looking at his
                own guts on the
                floor)
          Aah!!! OH MY GOD!!!

                    TECH THE TYRANT
          --GOD IS DEAD!!! THERE IS ONLY
          PAIN!!!---CHAOS!!!

TECH unties TOTINO and proceeds to drag him to a giant hook
that is hanging from the ceiling of the TORTURE-CHAMBER.

TECH THE TYRANT likes getting his hands not only dirty, but
bloody as well.

The madman hangs the half-alive VALTORE to the hook with his
organs in a matter of moments.

TECH steps back, and observes his tortuous work...

                    VALTORE TOTINO (CASINO OWNER)
               (dying)
          --They--they'll have your head for
          this...

                    TECH THE TYRANT
          --We shall see.

                                        CUT TO:

INT. 2017 HONDA CROSS-TOUR - MORNING

DR. ALEXANDER VEGAS drives through the strip...

He checks his side-view, and rear-view mirrors...scanning
them with his PURPLE-EYES as he coasts.

                    DR. ALEXANDER VEGAS
                (narrating,
                driving to work)
--LIFE'S NOT ABOUT HAVING THE WILL
TO WIN--IT'S ABOUT HAVING THE WILL
TO PREPARE TO WIN--Every fighter
must know, before he goes into a
fight, how the little fight fits
into the larger picture, and how
the evolution of his fighting will
decide the true-battle as a whole.
I make about $95K a year doing
what I do. I'm a Doctor, a
CHIROPRACTOR. I own VEGAS
CHIROPRACTICS. Even people that
gamble have back-problems believe
it or not. I don't gamble myself.
I was raised in LAS VEGAS, and my
Mom named me after this CITY OF
SIN. It's beautifully sinful and
sinfully beautiful. It never
sleeps, neither do I. I AM VEGAS.
I fix backs by day, and by
night...by night I fight. I
moonlight as a underground
MMA-fighter in what they call THE
UNDERWORLD FIGHT-CLUB. I make buku
doing it, too. I don't need the
money though. I just need the
rush. Fighting is freeing to me.
Some people smoke pot, some do
coke, some do yoga---I FIGHT. I
fight 7 days a week, always at
night. I just kind of got swept
into it. A lot of my
marine-buddies do it, and referred
me to it, and I've been fighting
every night for almost a year now,
I haven't lost a fight yet. I've
made nearly $250K doing it. It
helps pay the bills, and it's more
exciting than my day-job by leaps
and bounds.--When I'm Fighting, I
AM LIVING. It's an addiction for
me. I mean--who gets paid to
fight? It's a no-brainer for
me.---

DR. VEGAS gets to his office, he parks, exits his HONDA
CROSS-TOUR, and proceeds to enter the workplace.

He's white. 52 years old. VEGAS is extremely athletic for a
Doctor his age; about 6 ft 2.. Has short black hair, a beard

and moustache.

His purple-eyes are his most distinct feature. VEGAS is a rare-breed.

                                    CUT TO:

INT. VEGAS' CHIROPRACTICS OFFICE - DAY

VEGAS' assistant and secretary are more than ready to work. They greet the good Doctor with warmth and pure politeness as they always do.

VEGAS is good to his people---SARAH and MRS. BRETSKI are like his family.

DR. VEGAS has hardly any family left after his mother passed, they're distant and disconnected from him.

                    SARAH THE SECRETARY
                (flirtatiously
                 smiling at VEGAS)
            Hey, Alex.

                    MS. BRETSKI
            --Hello, Doc. How's your morning
            treating you?

                    DR. ALEXANDER VEGAS
            --So far so good, MS. BRETSKI, no
            complaints as of yet, how are you
            two?

SARAH THE SECRETARY is like a Nun--she's blonde, in her late 30s. She is mousy, quiet, yet very pretty--has green eyes that glow. She's a conservative lady.

                    SARAH THE SECRETARY
            --I just need a bit more coffee.

                    MS. BRETSKI
            --I'm good, Doc, finally got laid
            by my husband. It's been over 5
            months.

MRS. BRETSKI is in her late 50's, short, stubby and stubborn. She's a elderly saint of a woman. A marvelous assistant.

                    DR. ALEXANDER VEGAS
            MRS. BRETSKI, that's a little more
            than I needed to know.

                    MS. BRETSKI
--No Viagra, or anything. The wind
blew the right way, gave em a nice
erection.

                    SARAH THE SECRETARY
--I'm going to go make that coffee
now.--

                                        CUT TO:

INT. THE WAITING ROOM - LATER

A MAN, and 2 WOMEN are sitting in the waiting room of DR.
VEGAS' OFFICE, awaiting their treatment...

DR. VEGAS opens the door of his 'BACK-POPPING ROOM' and
calls for one of the patients: MR. ROYCE. A white man, 74
years old-even. Clean-shaven, buzzed cut. Yet, he's not too
aged to be elderly, he's spry. He gets up and walks toward
the doctor.

                    DR. ALEXANDER VEGAS
          --Mr. RAYMOND ROYCE, I'm Doctor
          Alex Vegas; come on in, good-sir.

                    MR. ROYCE
          --Alrighty then.

The two shake hands.

MR. ROYCE enters the room with VEGAS.

                                        CUT TO:

INT. THE BACK POPPING ROOM - CONTINUOUS

VEGAS examines ROYCE's paperwork and info...

He does so with a few quick glances.

                    DR. ALEXANDER VEGAS
          --Okay, Mr. Royce, it seems that,
          from what I can tell from your
          X-Ray results, your cervical,
          thoracic and your lumbar all are
          bent-out-of-shape. My Secretary
          said your pain levels are high.
          I'm gonna need you to lie down on
          this table here, we're going to
          make some adjustments today and
          over the course of several weeks.
                    (MORE)

                    DR. ALEXANDER VEGAS (cont'd)
          Does that sound okay, sir?

                    MR. ROYCE
          --Yes, sir, I just hope you can
          fix me.

ROYCE lies down on the padded table, uncomfortably so...

                    DR. ALEXANDER VEGAS
          I'll do my best, MR. ROYCE.

                    MR. ROYCE
          That's all any of us can do, huh?

There's a silence for a second.

                    MR. ROYCE
          --Which one is your secretary?

                    DR. ALEXANDER VEGAS
          The young one. The other, MRS.
          BRETSKI is my assistant.

                    MR. ROYCE
          --I thought secretaries answered
          phones, and assistants actually
          helped you with the work?

                    DR. ALEXANDER VEGAS
          Don't tell them that...hell.

VEGAS stands over ROYCE, and prepares to pop his back.

                    DR. ALEXANDER VEGAS
          Mr. Royce, inhale, please.

He does so, and VEGAS goes to pop ROYCE's back, all while
saying: "Now, Exhale"

We hear several snaps and crackles.

                    MR. ROYCE
          --Son-of-a-fuck, my back's tighter
          than my budget, Doc. Take it easy,
          will ya?

                    DR. ALEXANDER VEGAS
          --You a Marine, by any chance Mr.
          Royce?

                    MR. ROYCE
          --How can you tell?

                    DR. ALEXANDER VEGAS
--Your eyes. Semper Fi, Sir. I
served a few tours, here and
there.

                    MR. ROYCE
--Semper Fi. I was in 'Nam. 66-69.
          (raises pants leg
           up to show
           artificial leg)
--Vietcong got my fuckin' leg, and
I had to come back home. I
would've stayed and killed more of
'em, but what can ya do?

                    DR. ALEXANDER VEGAS
--Better to lose a leg than a
life.

                    MR. ROYCE
--Marines don't die, son.--

                    DR. ALEXANDER VEGAS
--No doubt, sir.
          (feels for the
           next spot to pop)
Now, breathe in for me another
good time, MR. ROYCE.

ROYCE does so.

VEGAS, as he pops his back, says: "Breathe Out"

                                        CUT TO:

INT. WAITING-ROOM - MOMENTS LATER

After having his back fiddled with, ROYCE exits the
BACK-POPPING ROOM.

                    MR. ROYCE
          (shakes VEGAS'
           hand)
-Thank you, Doctor VEGAS.

                    DR. ALEXANDER VEGAS
--You're welcome, Mr. Royce. All
you gotta do is go see my
assistant at the window, and
she'll get you set-up with another
appointment with me.

                    MR. ROYCE
          Alrighty, have a good day, son.

                    DR. ALEXANDER VEGAS
          You as well, sir.
               (grabs the file in
                the holder beside
                the door)
          Okay, next up, Ashley Rawlins.

A beautiful lady stands up, she is PATIENT 1. She enters the
room with DR. VEGAS.

                                        CUT TO:

INT. BACK-POPPING ROOM - CONTINUOUS

The DOCTOR examines her file, and even her...

                    DR. ALEXANDER VEGAS
          --You doing well today, MS.
          RAWLINS?--

                    PATIENT 1
               (hinting)
          --Yes, DOCTOR VEGAS. I'm swell, I
          just need my back--Broke, if you
          know what I mean...

PATIENT 1 gropes VEGAS.

He reacts unlike a typical man. He shuns her. He's no fag,
he just respects the Doctor-Patient relationship, which he
has never violated. He's been tested, and he's prevailed
sexually; he only makes love to women who are non-patients
is all.

                    DR. ALEXANDER VEGAS
               (getting the
                patient back)
          --Ma'am. I'm not that guy. I'm
          just not. Now, please lie down so
          I can do the necessary things to
          relieve your back-pain. If you
          won't, and you grope me again,
          I'll have to ask you to leave.
          That's just how this works...

                    PATIENT 1
          --Dammit. This makes me want you
          even more...

           DR. ALEXANDER VEGAS
What? Have you been stalking me?

              PATIENT 1
--No, I'm just a---I'm a
sex-addict. Please, excuse me,
sir. I really do have
back-problems, but it's
just---When I see a doctor,
especially one as handsome as you,
I go into an orgasmic-type of
shock. Forgive me.

           DR. ALEXANDER VEGAS
            (confused a bit)
Okay...let's get this over with
quickly. You have damage in the
lower regions of your spine. Lie
down, and we'll get this fixed up
as best we can. And, please, don't
be offended by my lack of desire
for you. I just absolutely don't
fuck patients. It's the
cardinal-rule.

              PATIENT 1
--Just pop my back, you fucking
queer.

She lies down.

VEGAS pops her back hurriedly.

A pop happens and we...

                       CUT TO:

INT. TECH'S HELICOPTER - CONTINUOUS

Looking spiffy in his attire, TECH, with a few shooters
rides in a black-military-helicopter.

TECH takes out an eye-drop-like vial full of a mysterious
substance, he drops the substance in both of his eyes as the
chopper lands.

              SHOOTER
--What the hell is that stuff
anyway, TECH?--I always forget to
ask.

                    TECH THE TYRANT
          --It's ADRENOCHROME. I always take
          it before a heist...gets the
          blood-pumpin'.

                    SHOOTER
          What the hell is adrenochrome,
          sir?

                    TECH THE TYRANT
               (dripping the drug
                into both of his
                eyes)
          It's adrenaline, extracted from
          the adrenal gland of the
          human-body. Yet it's in a
          customized form, when you drop it,
          it gets you higher than the
          heavens.

                    SHOOTER
          --Jesus Christ, you can't be
          serious?

                    TECH THE TYRANT
          --I am serious...and don't call me
          Jesus Christ. Now---Follow my
          lead.---

TECH's 6 SHOOTERS all shout: "Yes, Sir!" as they ready their
automatic weapons.

TECH and his guys exit the HELICOPTER.

                                        CUT TO:

EXT. THE DESERT - EVENING

                              LOCATION: APACHE
                              JUNCTION, ARIZONA

TECH THE TYRANT arrives to the scene of his own weapon's
deal...

The dealers are awaiting him about 35 yards away.

                    DEALER 1
               (looking at TECH'S
                HELICOPTER with
                pure disdain)
          --This fucking cock-sucker, who
          does he think he is being late
                    (MORE)

                   DEALER 1 (cont'd)
like this?!

                   DEALER 2
        (spits on the
        ground)
--Fuck 'Em. As long as he has the
cash...

                           CUT TO:

EXT. THE DESERT - MOMENTS LATER

TECH and his men walk up to the dealers, who have their
cases full of weaponry all ready to go.

Oddly, TECH and his crew have no ostensible cash on them.

                   TECH THE TYRANT
        (rubs his hands
        together)
--Hello, my friends. What do you
have for me???

DEALER 1 puts out his hand as a gesture to shake with TECH.

TECH ignores the gesture, and walks toward the weaponry; the
merchandise.

                   DEALER 2
--What we have is what you asked
for. Don't play coy with us,
TECHNO. We dealt with your father,
act as he would.

                   DEALER 1
--We could easily be dealing with
someone else.--Now, where's the
money? As you see, we have the
arms.

                   TECH THE TYRANT
--MY FATHER IS DEAD. So is my
Brother. I run both of their
operations. You fellas---you're
walking on glass and you're
cooking with gasoline; and I'ma
piss in ya vaseline. I'm not here
to buy your weapons, you measly
fools! I AM HERE TO TAKE THEM!!!

TECH waves his hand, and his SHOOTERS do work, emptying
their weapons at the other men, striking 3 of them dead.

There are only 9 men, including the 2 dealers.

The 2 dealers run for it. TECH chases them while his men
decease the remaining victims.

                                          CUT TO:

TECH THE TYRANT sprints himself, right after the 2 dealers.

He's a terrific athlete, and like a cheetah after gazelles,
TECH gains great ground on his prey.

He pulls a pistol and shoots both dealers in the back, while
still running.

The dealers fall to the ground.

                    TECH THE TYRANT
                 (standing over
                  dealer 1)
            You guys were runnin' like scalded
            dogs--WHY??? You cannot escape
            Death!!!

                    DEALER 2
                 (dying slowly,
                  bleeding out)
            --You think you can cross us???

                    DEALER 1
                 (coughing blood)
            --They'll have your fucking soul
            by the morning, you
            son-of-a-whore!!!

DEALER 1 pulls his pistol, and shoots at TECH.

TECH drops his pistol--he doesn't need it--he puts up his
metal arm, and blocks the bullets.

He walks up to DEALER 1 and breaks his neck.

TECH then walks up to DEALER 2, pulls a blade and stabs him
in the throat.

                    TECH THE TYRANT
                 (admiring his
                  "handy"-work)
            --I'm just gettin' started,
            fellas...you boys are my next
                    (MORE)

                         TECH THE TYRANT (cont'd)
        meal...

                                        CUT TO:

EXT. THE DESERT - MOMENTS LATER

TECH walks back from where he killed the two dealers.

                         SHOOTER
                --What's the word, sir?

                      TECH THE TYRANT
                --Gather those two bodies out
                there. I gotta extract them. And,
                get the weapons into the chopper.
                We gotta get back.

Having not checked the 2 vehicles of their victims, TECH and
Co. are ambushed by two shooters, who get out spraying and
praying.

TECH's SHOOTER kills one of the ambushing men.

TECH is close to the other. He grabs the man by the neck
with his metallic-hand. He picks him up off of his feet, and
squeezes him till he turns purple and dies.

                      TECH THE TYRANT
                   (walks toward his
                    helicopter)
                --Now---As I was saying, let's go.

The SHOOTERS all shout: "Yes, Sir!" and they proceed to
gather the weapons, etc.

                                        CUT TO:

INT. THE UNDERWORLD FIGHT-CLUB ARENA - NIGHT

                      DR. ALEXANDER VEGAS
                   (focused, on top
                    of his opponent
                    punching)

DOCTOR VEGAS BEATS HIS OPPONENT WITH TERRIFIC TENACITY.

                                   HE WINS THE BOUT BY
                                   KNOCK-OUT

A few hundred people are present in THE UNDERWORLD ARENA...

They are eating, drinking, chanting, reveling.

The FIGHT-CLUB is owned by: TECH THE TYRANT. It's his racket. Many computer-heads who enjoy MMA tune in through the Internet. Thousands upon thousands across the World. 10 Fights a night happen here in a CAGE. 1 Round. No Time Constraints. The victors are only victorious if they totally defeat or ultimately kill the opposing man...

DR. VEGAS is one fight away from becoming The Champion. He has just won, as he stands in the ring with his arm held up by the ref.

The Doctor's attire is an American-Flag Mouth-Piece, along with American-Flag-themed fighter-shorts; silk. His gloves are red. His shoes are blue. VEGAS suits up like he fights; all-out.

The crowd cheers him on.

ANNOUNCERS, sitting at a table with mics, like the UFC or WWE, are commentating as VEGAS exits the ring.

                    ANNOUNCER 1
          --ALEXANDER VEGAS, the Good Doctor
          with the win again folks.--

                    ANNOUNCER 2
          --What kind of doctor is he again?
          A Gynecologist, right?

                    ANNOUNCER 1
          --No, Bob, he's a Chiropractor.

                    ANNOUNCER 2
          --I always get those two mixed
          up...you know, he's gotta
          right-hook like RAY RICE...

                    ANNOUNCER 1
          --Now, BOB, that's just
          wrong.--Folks, we're ending on
          this fight, you all have a good
          night. Tune in tomorrow. Remember,
          "DON'T TALK ABOUT FIGHT CLUB". So
          we can stay in business, and the
          shadows. Be safe.---

                                        CUT TO:

INT. DR. VEGAS' HOME - LATER

VEGAS arrives to his pad. He enters.

It's not what you'd expect from a Dr. or a even a
prize-fighter.

It is very modest, discreet, and out of the way of all the
tumultuous nature of the metropolitan zone of VEGAS.

                                        CUT TO:

DR. VEGAS disrobes himself.

He walks around his house naked.

He goes to the fridge, and grabs some left-over Chinese
food; eating it, he goes to his cabinet and grabs some
WHISKEY.

He pops the top and chugs it a couple of times as he chews
his food.

                                        CUT TO:

30 MINUTES LATER

VEGAS exits the shower, gets dressed, and prepares himself
for his relaxation.

He leads a very isolated, quiet life. He has no pets, no
near relatives, he's completely alone...

The Good Doctor doses off...

                                        CUT TO:

EXT. THE JUNGLE - DAY

A PLATOON, lead by a COMMANDOR PORTNOY, are walking through
the jungle, calmly, quietly...

They're marines, on a mission in THE JUNGLE of SOUTH
AMERICA. This is a recon-mission, taking out a
CARTEL-leader.

Behind PORTNOY is then SERGEANT ALEXANDER VEGAS...

                    SOLDIER 1
              --COMMANDOR, our visibility is
              shit out here. You sure we're
              headed to 'Charlie'?

                    COMMANDOR PORTNOY
--You ass, you're like a kid: "Are
we there yet?", that's how you
sound. I'm about to have you tied
to a tree with your fucking mouth
taped.--

                    SOLDIER 2
          (to Vegas)
--Hey, Boss, look what I found.

                    SERGEANT VEGAS
          (turns to see
          SOLDIER 2)
--Damn, you found pot out here?
You might not wanna take that.

                    SOLDIER 2
          (sarcastic,
           stuffing
           marijuana plants
           in his pants)
-It's like a sore dick: you can't
beat it. Ima use it for camo
too.--

                    SERGEANT VEGAS
          (to PORTNOY)
--Sir?--

                    COMMANDOR PORTNOY
--What is it, VEGAS?

                    SERGEANT VEGAS
--Is this really your last
mission?--That's the word goin'
around.

                    COMMANDOR PORTNOY
--Yes, it is, son. How many
sons-of-bitches we put down
together?

                    SERGEANT VEGAS
--Masses, sir...--Why are you
giving it up, you're not aged
out?--

                    COMMANDOR PORTNOY
Life is a fight, VEGAS. I feel
like I'm losing, and more risk
goes into it being in places like
this. I'm ready to be a civilian
again. I feel like--like I been
                    (MORE)

                    COMMANDOR PORTNOY (cont'd)
          shot at and missed, shit at and
          hit, you know???--

                    SERGEANT VEGAS
          --Well, sir, me and the boys are
          gonna throw you a retirement party
          as soon as---

As they walk through the JUNGLE, bullets string across at
the soldiers...

They scatter, and take their respective positions...

A couple of the PLATOON-members are killed instantly as
machine gun-fire rains upon them. THEY'RE SURROUNDED by 20
or so CARTEL-ASSASSINS.

                    COMMANDOR PORTNOY
          --Return Fire!!!--

PORTNOY, VEGAS, and CO. return plenty of bullets back to the
CARTEL-members, quite successfully.

They quickly eradicated the threat, they spread, and
converge on all their enemies.

As the others sweep and clear the petty, sloppy assassins,
VEGAS and PORTNOY check on their fallen members.

                    SERGEANT VEGAS
                (runs to his
                 fallen brother)
          --You son-of-a-bitch, don't you
          fucking dare die on me!!!
                (tries to revive
                 him)
          --Fuck!!!

                    COMMANDOR PORTNOY
                (stands over his
                 fallen comrade)
          --Lord Jesus, bless my dead.--
                (shakes his head)
          Guys, we gotta---

An unseen sniper takes fire at PORTNOY from a tree-top-post,
blowing his face clean off...

VEGAS runs to his aid, as do the others, but PORTNOY is like
VEGAS' father. They've been through thick and thin together
in the service.

                    SERGEANT VEGAS
                 (lunges at PORTNOY
                  to check on him)
              --Sir!?--COMMANDOR?!!!
                   (yells at the
                    bloody sight)
                --NO!!!--

VEGAS, purple eyes glowing, picks up his weapon, and fires
unrelentingly at the sniper's post in the tree-top 35 yards
off.

He destroys the tree-top post, and the sniper falls to the
ground riddled with bullets but breathing still.

VEGAS charges his fallen enemy...

                     SOLDIER 2
                --VEGAS! Wait!

Alexander Vegas stands over the Cartel-shooter and proceeds
to beat him to death with his fists.

                    SERGEANT VEGAS
                   (roaring
                    powerfully)
                --Aah!!!

He beats the man's face in, literally.

His teammates try to hold him back, but VEGAS cannot be
stopped. He decimates the shooter with his bare-hands.

We see a punch, and we:

                                            CUT TO:

EXT. DREAM-STATE/THE BEACH - DAY

A young, still purple-eyed, ALEXANDER VEGAS, boyish,
youthful, is running on the beach. He's running toward
someone...

The sand is softer than fresh-snow, making it extremely
difficult to run.

He still proceeds.

                                            CUT TO:

A figure is at the end of the beach, just standing there.
It's a woman.

                         VEGAS' MOTHER
                        (turns around)
              My Little Alexander The Great...
                        (stretches her
                         hand out to her
                         son)
              Come, sit with me.

                         YOUNG VEGAS
              Mom??? What are you doing here?
              Where are we?

VEGAS tries to grab his mother's hand, but cannot.

As he does so, quick-sand starts absorbing him into the
ground.

                         VEGAS' MOTHER
              I LOVE YOU, Son.

He sinks into the ground, consumed by the quick-sand.

                         YOUNG VEGAS
                        (being consumed by
                         the quick-sand)
              Aah!!!

A hand can be felt by VEGAS, it's lifting him up out of the
sand.

The hand pulls VEGAS up out of the sand, yet now he's a
grown man...

                         TECH THE TYRANT
                        (holding VEGAS up
                         out of the
                         quick-sand)
              --You ever FIGHT with God by the
              bright Sun-Light???

                         DR. ALEXANDER VEGAS
              Huh???

With his robotic-Red-eyes, TECH sees into DR.
VEGAS.---Holding VEGAS with one of his metal arms, TECH THE
TYRANT reaches his other metal-arm into VEGAS' torso and
feels around...

He can feel the pain.

                         DR. ALEXANDER VEGAS
              --Aah!!!---

114

                    TECH THE TYRANT
                (prying VEGAS'
                 stomach open)
            --You have something that belongs
            to me...

                                    CUT TO:

INT. VEGAS' HOME - MORNING

VEGAS' eyes shoot open, he's utterly distraught.

                    DR. ALEXANDER VEGAS
                (breathing heavy)
            Un-fucking-real...

The DOCTOR gathers his bearings, and proceeds to get ready
for work.

                    DR. ALEXANDER VEGAS
            --When I lost my mom, it was one
            of the worst things to happen to
            me. She passed due to a stroke
            when I was a teenager. She was my
            best-friend. She raised me all by
            herself; told me my dad died
            serving his country. Died a
            marine. My mother--she never
            expected anything from anybody.
            She instilled my work ethic in me.
            She's the reason I went to UCLA to
            practice medicine. I know she'd be
            proud of me. The way she was in my
            dream was so real, like she was
            telling me something. The guy with
            the metal-arms? I have no idea
            what that's about. I'm big on
            dreams. I try to remember 'em all.
            But, I just can't.--

                                    CUT TO:

INT. RESTAURANT - MORNING

DR. VEGAS is eating with SARAH and MS. BRETSKI.

They're having a big-breakfast, with coffee, before heading
in for a long day's work.

VEGAS has a scratch under his eye, nothing significant, yet
it's noticable.

                    MS. BRETSKI
--ALEX, what the hell you get
into? Why do ya got that cut on
your face?

                    DR. ALEXANDER VEGAS
I got a--I got a kitten yesterday.
Damn thing clawed me is all.--

                    SARAH THE SECRETARY
--The pussy got to ya, huh?

                    DR. ALEXANDER VEGAS
--Sarah, I appreciate the
innuendo, but trust me, I'm not
sleeping with any of these Vegas
women. If most of these women
around here had as many dicks
stickin' out of 'em as they have
inside of 'em, they'd look like a
damn porcupine.

VEGAS sips his coffee, as SARAH and MS. BRETSKI sit in utter
shock by the misogynistic comment.

                    DR. ALEXANDER VEGAS
               (slurping his
                coffee)
--What? It's the truth...

                                        CUT TO:

INT. BACK-POPPING ROOM - LATER

DR. VEGAS lets a PATIENT into the BACK-POPPING-ROOM.

                    DR. ALEXANDER VEGAS
Hello, Mr. Douche, I'm Dr. Vegas.
It's a pleasure to meet you. How
are we today?

                    GHETTO
--Bruh, don't call me by my
'government'...

                    DR. ALEXANDER VEGAS
Okay, sir. I work with all my new
patients as far as names. What
would you like me to call you?

                         GHETTO
                  (with a low-tone,
                   speaking quickly)
              --Call me "Ghetto".--

Dr. Vegas mishears the man...

                    DR. ALEXANDER VEGAS
              Okay, 'Calmagetto'. If you'll lie
              down on the table, I'll---

                         GHETTO
              No, Bruh. I said CALL ME 'GHETTO'!

                    DR. ALEXANDER VEGAS
                  (shakes his head
                   in understanding)
              --Now, I see, brother-man. We got
              some work to do on ya today. Lie
              down, please...

The PATIENT is dumbfounded by the Doctor's lack of fear of
his "blackness", but he still listens to VEGAS.

                                        CUT TO:

INT. THE WAITING-ROOM - LATER

The aggressive PATIENT leaves the back-popping room. VEGAS
sticks his head out, and calls for the next...

                    DR. ALEXANDER VEGAS
              --Mr. Royce, you're up, sir.

RAYMOND ROYCE gets up and proceeds to enter the back-popping
room with VEGAS.

                         MR. ROYCE
              --Alrighty, how you doing there,
              Doc?--

                    DR. ALEXANDER VEGAS
              --Quite well, sir, no complaints
              as of yet.

DR. VEGAS shuts the door.

                                        CUT TO:

INT. BACK-POPPING ROOM - CONTINUOUS

VEGAS looks over ROYCE's chart to see what adjustments need to be made.

> DR. ALEXANDER VEGAS
> --If you'd lie down on your stomach, MR. ROYCE, we're going to iron out the kinks for ya.

> MR. ROYCE
> Just be careful, Doc. My damn GIZZARD is killin' me...gotta get it took out soon.

> DR. ALEXANDER VEGAS
> --Your Gizzard?

> MR. ROYCE
> Yep, the doc said I don't need it no more. It's just taking up space.

> DR. ALEXANDER VEGAS
> (chuckles)
> --You mean Gallbladder, I think, Mr. Royce.

> MR. ROYCE
> (lays down on the table)
> Yeah--that's it.

VEGAS prepares ROYCE for his popping.

> DR. ALEXANDER VEGAS
> Okay, Mr. Royce, breathe in...

ROYCE takes a deep breath.

DR. VEGAS pops his back.

> MR. ROYCE
> --Damn, son. That was a major pop!

> DR. ALEXANDER VEGAS
> Yes, sir, it was. Now just breathe in one more time.

> MR. ROYCE
> --Hold on, Doc. Hey, can I borrow some money from ya?

                    DR. ALEXANDER VEGAS
          That depends, sir. How much?

                    MR. ROYCE
                 (smirking)
          --All ya got'll do.--

                    DR. ALEXANDER VEGAS
          I'm sure it would, MR. ROYCE. Now,
          breathe in.

VEGAS pops his back, and tells ROYCE to: "Breathe out"

                    MR. ROYCE
          How'd you get the purple eyes,
          man? Contacts?

                    DR. ALEXANDER VEGAS
          Nah, they're not contacts. I don't
          know really. My eyes are just
          purple...

                    MR. ROYCE
          You look like a alien or something
          with them things. Not in a bad
          way...just never seen purple eyes
          is all.

                    DR. ALEXANDER VEGAS
          That's understandable. Now,
          breathe in again for me please,
          sir.

ROYCE does so. VEGAS pops his back...

                                        CUT TO:

INT. WAITING-ROOM - CONTINUOUS

VEGAS opens his door to let out MR. ROYCE.

ROYCE doesn't exit immediately however.

                    MR. ROYCE
                 (turns around to
                  face VEGAS)
          --How about you and I hit up a bar
          sometime? Share war-stories?

                    DR. ALEXANDER VEGAS
          --Well, sir, that'd be kinda
          negating doctor/patient
          relations---I don't---

                    MR. ROYCE
          It's not a request, son. It's an
          order. Be at the BAR on Sapphire
          Street at 10 PM sharp, tonight.

VEGAS is beat. He has to follow orders...

                    DR. ALEXANDER VEGAS
          --Yes, sir. We can do that. I got
          something at 1 AM, but that
          shouldn't infringe.---

                    MR. ROYCE
          Good, now you have a good day,
          doc. I'm outta here.

ROYCE goes to the SECRETARY'S WINDOW to check out.

VEGAS calls in his next patient.

                                        CUT TO:

INT. THE SECRETARY'S WINDOW - MOMENTS LATER

ROYCE, with charisma, walks up to the window to setup his
next appointment.

                    MS. BRETSKI
          Okay, Mr. Royce, will this
          upcoming Friday be a good day for
          you to come back in?

                    MR. ROYCE
          Yes, ma'am. Make it early in the
          day too, please.

                    MS. BRETSKI
          9 AM sound good?

                    MR. ROYCE
          That'll do, ma'am.

ROYCE takes MS. BRETSKI's pen.

                    MR. ROYCE
               (with the pen
                in-hand)
          The Doctor told me to take
                    (MORE)

                    MR. ROYCE (cont'd)
something...

                    MS. BRETSKI
You can't have my pen, sir.

                    MR. ROYCE
Well, that's just too bad.
          (puts the pen back)
Just foolin' with ya, darlin'. You
have a nice day. I'll be here
Friday at 2.

ROYCE exits the office.

                              CUT TO:

INT. THE BAR - NIGHT

DR. VEGAS sits casually at a BAR-BOOTH, awaiting the arrival
of ROYCE.

ROYCE enters, he hobbles to the booth that VEGAS is at.

                    DR. ALEXANDER VEGAS
     --Hello, Sir.--

                    MR. ROYCE
     --Hello, Son.---

MR. ROYCE takes his artificial leg off the amputated area,
and sits the leg upward, beside him in the booth.

VEGAS is caught off guard.

                    DR. ALEXANDER VEGAS
     Can't you put that thing
     horizontal?

                    MR. ROYCE
     --Nah, I want people to know I got
     a weapon at my disposal. A robber
     tries something, I'll hit 'em with
     this here leg two good times,
     lights out...if I lay it down,
     it'll be harder to retrieve, you
     know?

                    DR. ALEXANDER VEGAS
     --I see your logic, sir, honestly.
     These days, they're bad, huh?

                    MR. ROYCE
          --No shit! You got Russians
          everywhere, radical Islamists,
          TYRANTS...all of whom want to
          destroy our Home, our Country!
          Nobody trusts anybody anymore, the
          whole society is corroded to the
          point that deception and
          destruction are the most common
          expression of most folks these
          days.--

                    DR. ALEXANDER VEGAS
          --You're smarter than you let on,
          ROYCE...

                    MR. ROYCE
          Son, if you only knew...

A cute WAITER approaches the two soldiers. She has a
wonderful, vibrant smile.

                    WAITER
          --What can I get you two gentlemen
          tonight?

                    MR. ROYCE
          --Jack, on the rocks.--

                    DR. ALEXANDER VEGAS
          --Cranberry Juice, please, no
          liquor for me.

                    MR. ROYCE
          --What are you havin' vaginal
          cramps? Get a real drink, pussy.

The WAITER's smile, turns into her jaw almost dropping to
the floor by the words of ROYCE.

                    DR. ALEXANDER VEGAS
                (to ROYCE)
          --Can't do it, sir, I got business
          to attend to later tonight. One
          drink, for me, leads to 10.
                (to the WAITER)
          --Cranberry Juice will do, Ma'am.
          Thank you.

                    WAITER
          --Coming right up.--

The WAITER goes to prepare the men's drinks.

122

                    MR. ROYCE
--Damn, if I'd known you wasn't
drinkin', we could've went
elsewhere. Not drinkin' at a bar
is like not fuckin' in an orgy.
It's not right.

                    DR. ALEXANDER VEGAS
That's one way of putting it.
So--where you from ROYCE?

                    MR. ROYCE
Here, VEGAS. I grew up here before
it exploded, and became what it is
now. Nowadays, it seems like "LOST
VEGAS". I left to go to
war---lived in DC for awhile when
I returned. I contracted for some
agencies for a bit, white-collar.
But, I'm back in the city that
sins. I missed it here. I missed
everything...

                    DR. ALEXANDER VEGAS
We got some parallels in that
regard. Both' us being from VEGAS,
servin' an' all, and then comin'
back. But, I just fought, never
contracted with anybody or worked
on the other side. It's cool
meetin' a vet of your caliber.

                    MR. ROYCE
--Well, it's the life I
chose...really it chose me. Once
you're in, you're in when you did
it as long as I did. But, on to
another tale...you know, you're
the only chiropractor in town
worth a damn? I been to three
already, and they just ruined my
back even more.

                    DR. ALEXANDER VEGAS
--Being a Chiropractor is the best
thing that's ever happened to me,
post-military. It keeps me
grounded, stable, from all the
CHAOS of life.

                    MR. ROYCE
--You got the touch, kid, you do
good work as a Chiropractor, my
back is already doing wonders. I
                    (MORE)

                    MR. ROYCE (cont'd)
appreciate how you're helping me
out.

                    DR. ALEXANDER VEGAS
--Well, that means a lot, sir,
truly.--

The WAITER returns with their drinks...

                    WAITER
               (placing the
               drinks on the
               table to VEGAS
               and ROYCE)
--Enjoy, gentlemen.--

VEGAS and ROYCE say in-sync: "Yes, Ma'am."

                    DR. ALEXANDER VEGAS
--She reminds me of my mother...

                    MR. ROYCE
--How so? And, where's your mother
now?

                    DR. ALEXANDER VEGAS
               (nostalgic)
She just has that spunk like Mom,
but Mom--She's passed on...

                    MR. ROYCE
               (deeply saddened)
--I'm sorry to hear that...

Both the men down their drinks at the same time, chugging.

                    DR. ALEXANDER VEGAS
               (contemplating)
--Sir, I--I need to go now...I'll
go to the cash-register and cover
our drinks and the tip, but I have
to go...

                    MR. ROYCE
               (concerned)
--Where to, son?--

                    DR. ALEXANDER VEGAS
               (with
               determination in
               his voice)
--TO FIGHT.--

                                        CUT TO:

INT. ROYCE'S HOME - LATER

ROYCE enters his small-home, right outside of the metropolis
of VEGAS...

He shuts the door, and looks at his mail.

                    MR. ROYCE
              (looking at one of
               the mail items)
         --Well, what do we have here?--

One of the letters is from DR. VEGAS himself, courtesy of
VEGAS CHIROPRACTICS.

ROYCE reads the letter. It reads as follows:

August 20th, 2018

RAYMOND ROYCE
133 ARCHIE DR.
LAS VEGAS, NV
89104

RE: Account 10530

Thank you for the confidence you have shown by choosing me
as your CHIROPRACTOR. I appreciate the opportunity to work
with you on the road to good health.

I want you to understand what we are trying to accomplish
together. First, Webster defines a symptom as "something
that indicates the existence of something else". The pain
and discomfort that brought you to my office is a symptom,
an indication you have a problem. The pain itself is not
your problem. Our approach is to correct the underlying
cause of your problem through specific spinal adjustments.

Second, the healing process takes time. Many times the
problem has existed for months or even years. While some
patients experience relief after only a few adjustments, the
corrective process has just begun. If you terminate the
adjustments once the pain is gone, the problem may not be
corrected yet. On the other hand, if you do not experience
immediate relief, do not get discouraged. Your body is
unique; it will heal on its own time table.

Third, there are some things that you can do to speed your
recovery process. I will be giving you specific exercises
and stretches for your condition. Also, there are

nutritional-supplements you could take to speed recovery and improve overall health and well being.

If you are interested in this service, speak with me during your next visit.

I am pleased and excited that you have chosen to become healthy through 'VEGAS CHIROPRACTICS'. It's the natural road to good health.

Yours in Health,

ALEXANDER VEGAS, DC

The letter is signed by the doctor himself, with a fancy signature to match the name.

                    MR. ROYCE
               (shaken)
          --Wow. Just, wow.--

                                        CUT TO:

ROYCE puts the letter down and reacts unexpectedly. A couple tears fall from his eyes.

MR. ROYCE recoups himself, and moves to his open-computer, which is processing information, loading various files on none-other than: TECH THE TYRANT...

                    MR. ROYCE
               (scanning his
                computer's
                processes,
                referring to TECH)
          --The TYRANT must fall, or MY CITY
          will die.---

                                        CUT TO:

INT. THE SHED - MORNING

                                        YEAR: 1991

Ice shakes, making the sound of a back-popping.

BRODY BARNES, and his sons are preparing their caught fish for cleaning.

BRODY places the cooler on his cleaning table, as his children watch him start the cleansing process...

They watch his every move.

>   BRODY BARNES
>   (pulls a blade)
>   --Like some men, some fish have to
>   be gutted...

BRODY, with his blade, cuts the head off of the specimen,
and rips its guts out, while also cutting out the asshole of
the creature; all required to clean a fish properly for
consumption.

>   BRODY BARNES
>   (with bloody hands)
>   --Sometimes, your prey must be
>   mutilated.---Beings who refuse to
>   kill will themselves be mutilated.
>   Beings who refuse to get their
>   hands dirty, will themselves be
>   dirtied with hands. Do you
>   understand me, my sons?

BRODY BARNES disposes of the guts and things of the fish.

He grabs another from the cooler, slams it on the
cleaning-table, and he cuts the head off.

The knife hits the board as the fishes head disconnects, and
we CUT TO:

INT. THE UNDERWORLD FIGHT CLUB ARENA - NIGHT

A couple hours after having chatted with MR. ROYCE, DR.
VEGAS is standing toe-to-toe with an opponent in the ring;
an opponent far more formidable than he.

He is digesting punches, left-and-right, while also dishing
the same. It's a stalemate at this point.

>   DR. ALEXANDER VEGAS
>   (fatigued,
>   fighting harder
>   than ever)

VEGAS backs up, regathering himself for an attack.

He does so with haste. He moves backward, realigns himself
and goes for the "Superman-Punch".

He lands it, but it only pisses his opponent off.

                    OPPONENT 2
                 (takes the hit,
                  charges VEGAS)
              --Aah!!!--

OPPONENT 2 jukes to the side of VEGAS, and he jumps onto the
cage, and runs on it...VEGAS' opponent then performs a
running-jump-kick off of the cage.

This blow knocks the doctors mouthpiece out and lays him out
on the mat.

He falls into a deep slumber...

ANNOUNCER 1 sits at the table right outside of the cage...

                    ANNOUNCER 1
              --Wow, a lot of folks just lost a
              lot of loot. The good doctor is
              out, folks.---

ANNOUNCER 2 shows up just in time, puts his headset back on
ready to do some "announcing"...

                    ANNOUNCER 2
                 (without headset,
                  distorted)
              --Chiropractors aren't doctors!--

                    ANNOUNCER 1
              --Where in the hell were you,
              Bob?--

                    ANNOUNCER 2
              --I was fucking your wife in the
              back.--

                    ANNOUNCER 1
              --You were gone for no more than a
              minute.

                    ANNOUNCER 2
              --Exactly.--

                    ANNOUNCER 1
              --Well, somebody's gotta do it.--

                                        CUT TO:

INT. THE COUNT-ROOM - CONTINUOUS

Naked women are in THE COUNT-ROOM, quantifying TECH THE
TYRANT's loot from those that bet on his fights.

There's piles of money being handled by the counters...

A woman drops a dollar...

                    COUNTER 1
          --Honey, you just started here,
          it's okay if you fuck up the first
          day...just don't let it be a
          habit, or THE TYRANT will get
          you...

                    COUNTER 2
          --The who?--

                    COUNTER 1
          --TECHNO. TECH. He sees all, he
          knows all. He's our Boss. We count
          for him. Part man, part
          machine--he--HE IS OUR KING.---

                    COUNTER 2
          I don't even wanna know, girl. I'm
          just here to feed my family...

                    COUNTER 1
          --You'll know soon enough, my
          dear.--He is the most dangerous
          man on the planet.

The unclothed women count away, fearfully, precisely.

                                        CUT TO:

INT. THE LOCKER-ROOM - MOMENTS LATER

Out of breath, beaten, defeated, downtrodden, DR. VEGAS sits
on a bench in the locker-room, it is empty, only he is
there.

He looks in the top of his locker, where his payment should
be...

It is not there. No money is there.

                    DR. ALEXANDER VEGAS
          --What the fuck?--

THE MONEY MAN enters, silently, coldly.

                    DR. ALEXANDER VEGAS
          --Am I not gettin' paid, guy?
          What's going on? The non-victors
          get payment too. I've not lost a
          fight with you people til now.--I
          should get my usual rate.

                    MONEY MAN
          --Your skills are no longer needed
          here. We're terminating your
          position as a fighter with us, MR.
          VEGAS.

                    DR. ALEXANDER VEGAS
          --It's Doctor.---And, I want my
          fuckin' money.

                    MONEY MAN
          Take it up with the TYRANT...I
          dare you...

THE MONEY MAN backs into the shadows and disappears from THE
LOCKER ROOM.

                    DR. ALEXANDER VEGAS
               (punches the
                walls, the
                lockers, goes
                ape-shit)
          FUCK!!!

                                        CUT TO:

INT. THE ROOM OF SCREENS - LATER

TECH is up and about, listening, looking at the power...the
information.

A WOMAN enters THE ROOM OF SCREENS. TECH never leaves there
really, unless he's conducting some-type of business,
money-or-death-wise.

The WOMAN who has entered is his woman. She is: MIA
MAELSTROM

Her hair is dark as black-tar. Her eyes are the same. No
White is in them, just blackness.

She is tiny, Hispanic, exquisite, yet she is scarred badly;
almost Stigmata-like. There is evidence of torture to her;

she has scars, from needle-points all over, looking as if she's been shot or pierced hundreds of times.

Her face is pretty, but damaged; TECH put her through the ringer, and made her his personal lap-dog, making her think he loves her. She does what he says with pleasure; the Stockholm syndrome is strong with MIA. She's been brainwashed to do TECH's bidding, fuck him, and that's about it.

                    MIA MAELSTROM
          --I handled the hit, mi amor.--I
          also made out with 50K. He gave it
          to me before tasting my blade.

                    TECH THE TYRANT
               (walks up to her)
          Very good, MIA.
               (kisses MIA)
          Your proficiency never ceases to
          amaze me. Your elegance is matched
          by your deadliness, my sweet.

                    MIA MAELSTROM
          What is the next task for us?

                    TECH THE TYRANT
               (kisses MIA's hand)
          Around 3AM, we hit TOTINO's
          CASINO. They're expecting him, not
          us. We're going to take it for the
          throwaway cash to float us till we
          control the city in its finality.
          While my guys handle that, you
          will take care of the bosses. WE
          WILL CONTROL LAS VEGAS, and when
          we do, my dear, you will be THE
          QUEEN OF IT.
               (turns and looks
                at the screens)
          But, right this moment, I must
          wreak CHAOS on the people, so they
          then can be controlled. Watch,
          MIA---THE TERROR...
               (his red-eyes
                interface with
                his computers)
          --God didn't create man
          equal...TECHNOLOGY DID...

TECH begins hacking the US Military's primary network, with ease...

MIA, smiling, puts her hand on TECH's shoulder as he goes "to town", and gears up for his CYBER-ATTACK.

>   TECH THE TYRANT
>   --KARMA, break down any-and-all
>   firewalls that I cannot,
>   understood?

>   KARMA THE A.I
>   --Yes, Boss. I am on it.

>   TECH THE TYRANT
>   --I'm hacking their mainframe now,
>   just keep them off my scent,
>   KARMA. I just need 30 more
>   seconds, and I'll own the US
>   MILITARY MAINFRAME for about, ah,
>   30 minutes. That's all the time I
>   need though.

>   CUT TO:

EXT. LOS ANGELES/METROPOLITAN AREA - LATER

FAST CUTS:

UNMANNED DRONES, HACKED BY TECH, begin destroying the city of LA.

The drones are weaponized...missiles, and machine gun fire are going off all over as the mindless machines, controlled by the masochistic cyber-terrorist, TECH, are attacking relentlessly.

People are getting blown to bits, being torn to shreds by the multitude of drones. Runnin' or not, people are perishing, left-and-right.

>   CUT TO:

All the traffic-lights in LA turn Red.

All vehicles stop, making them easier targets...

Out-of-nowhere, random explosions start happening.

TECH THE TYRANT has managed to hack into the cellular-phone grid of LA, turning people's phones into explosive devices.

Thousands of phone-bombs go off, killing thousands of innocents...

                                              CUT TO:

EXT. LAS VEGAS STRIP - LATER

DR. VEGAS is walking toward his car from the UNDERWORLD
FIGHT ARENA.

He is on the strip, it's actually quiet on this night. Not
many folks present, no police presence.

Not much occurring on the scene, till now.

                                              CUT TO:

Stopping in his tracks, DR. VEGAS sees a 'BADGER'-mini-tank,
rolling fast toward the entrance of a CASINO, followed by a
white-van out of which exits 4 SHOOTERS, heavily armed.

VEGAS ducks to avoid being seen.

                                              CUT TO:

EXT. TOTINO'S CASINO - MORNING

TIME: AROUND 3 AM

The BADGER TANK destroys the entrance, the gunmen enter and
lay waste to all the people inside in a few moments...

They're trained assassins.

3 MINUTES ELAPSE:

Leaving the BADGER behind, the men exit TOTINO's CASINO with
briefcases full of cash.

They put the cases in the white-van. People run in panic,
police fail to respond to the heist, oddly.

                                              CUT TO:

EXT. THE STRIP - CONTINUOUS

DR. VEGAS, stupidly reveals himself.

                          DR. ALEXANDER VEGAS
                    --Now, I've watched a lot of
                    heist-movies in my day, but this
                    beats 'em all--that was
                    one-hell-of a robbery, there,
                              (MORE)

                         DR. ALEXANDER VEGAS (cont'd)
     guys.

Caught-off-guard, the gunmen, and TECH's BODYGUARD, who was
driving the mini-tank, all turn to face VEGAS with their
weapons pointed, ready to kill.

                         THE BODYGUARD
     --Who the hell are you?

                         DR. ALEXANDER VEGAS
     --I'm just a Doctor, fellas.
               (walks with his
                hands up toward
                the SHOOTERS and
                THE BODYGUARD)
     --I'm also from here. From VEGAS.
     And, I'm not going to allow you
     guys to leave here without paying
     for your massacre...I've seen a
     lot of war in my day, but not in
     my town, good sirs, and I will not
     stand for this.

                         SHOOTER 2
               (laughing)
     Ha-ha-ha

                         SHOOTER 1
     --Man, get the fuck out of here.

                         THE BODYGUARD
     --Shoot 'em.--

                         SHOOTER 4
     --With pleasure.

DR. VEGAS gestures to the men to not fire.

                         DR. ALEXANDER VEGAS
     --Wait, why don't all of you
     just--FIGHT ME?

                         SHOOTER 3
               (drops his weapon)
     --Let's stomp his ass out!--

They all drop their weapons, they refuse to negate the
challenge...

They charge VEGAS.

The good DOCTOR grabs SHOOTER 1 by the throat and rips his

Adam's-Apple out, while at the same time kicking the
bodyguard in the face so hard it breaks 5 of his teeth.

                              CUT TO:

DR. VEGAS collapses in SHOOTER 2's knee by kicking it
inward. The man falls to the ground and VEGAS stomps his
face in.

SHOOTER 3 and 4 try to restrain VEGAS as THE BODYGUARD
gathers his bearings.

The CHIROPRACTOR breaks free from the SHOOTERS and breaks
one's sternum, while dislocating the other's jaw.

                              CUT TO:

THE BODYGUARD attacks VEGAS with all he's got.

The Chiropractor kills him with one punch.

He then picks up one of the guns, and puts bullets into all
of the men, already deceased or no, just to be certain and
JUST...

                              CUT TO:

ALEX VEGAS looks around, no cops in sight. Those not dead
have fled.

He does what any man would do. He takes one of the
briefcases full of cash, and takes off from THE CHAOS.

                              CUT TO:

INT. THE ROOM OF SCREENS - LATER

TECH, sipping blood and eating brains, sits in his ROOM OF
SCREENS, waiting patiently for any news.

                    KARMA THE A.I
          Boss?

                    TECH THE TYRANT
          Yes, KARMA?

                    KARMA THE A.I
          -_I have something you need to
          see. Your--your job, it went south
          in a big way.

                    TECH THE TYRANT
          --Show me...what's wrong, KARMA?

                    KARMA THE A.I
          Showing feed now.

KARMA provides the footage of VEGAS thwarting the CASINO
Robbery.

He's quite stunned by VEGAS' ability.

                    TECH THE TYRANT
          He's gotta be a fighter...

                    KARMA THE A.I
          He is, Boss. His name is Alexander
          Vegas.

                    TECH THE TYRANT
          --God, I love irony.--Thank you
          for updating me. MIA and I will
          handle him.

                              CUT TO:

INT. THE CASINO BOSSES' HEADQUARTERS - LATER

The CASINO OWNERS, BOSSES, are having a secret meeting.
They're chatting about percentages, intakes, cash-flow of
their respective properties and what not...

Little do they know, they're on the verge of meeting
death...

                    ROGER BURESS (CASINO OWNER)
                    (mid-discussion)
          --You and all the rest of ya' know
          that we're on a steady decline.
          Revenues are shit for all of us
          this Quarter. What the hell are we
          going to do? We've been hacked,
          robbed, our guys are getting shot
          down during transfers like dogs!!!
          What in the living-fuck are you
          gonna do, GALBONI?! I need
          assurances, and you ain't
          providing shit! This--THIS TECH
          THE TYRANT, or whoever-the-fuck is
          raping us for every damn dime on
          the dollar!!!--

                    ARCHIE GALBONI (CASNIO OWNER LEADER)
          --I empathize with your concern as
          you know I've been made a victim
          in this conspiracy too. The
          guy--TECH, BRODY's kid, he's a
          Monster...I have no plays to make
          with this son-of-a-bastard. He's
          too smart. For all I know, he's
          listening in to us right this
          moment...maybe we should pool our
          resources to find and kill 'em.
          That's all I really know to do,
          fellas.

                    ANTHONY FALCON (CASINO OWNER)
               (red-faced)
          ---I'VE LOST OVER $35 MILLION
          DOLLARS BECAUSE OF THAT
          MOTHERFUCKER and his fight club!!!
          I WANT HIM DEAD! NOW, ARCHIE!
          RIGHT FUCKING N---

MIA MAELSTROM storms into the meeting quite threateningly,
unannounced...

The beautiful warrior of a woman unsheathes her SAMURAI
SWORD; it has a golden-blade, composed of the hardest
earthly metals, a handle made of pure titanium-alloy, yet it
is not a flashy sword...it is a weapon of death. A sword
forged for destruction.

                    ROGER BURESS (CASINO OWNER)
               (astonished by MIA
               MAELSTROM)
          --Who in the flying-fuck are you
          supposed to be, Lady?!

                    MIA MAELSTROM
               (stoical)
          --I---I AM CHAOS...

She goes to work on the CASINO BOSSES.

She decapitates ROGER BURESS as he gets up to contest her.

The others try to evacuate, but she is blocking the only way
out.

MIA MAELSTROM vertically slices ANTHONY FALCON. SLICES HIM
IN HALF, literally.

The others, besides ARCHIE, get their faces, simultaneously,
sliced wide open...

ARCHIE's all that's left. The men's guards were slain so silently...the OWNERS are no match for Ms. MAELSTROM...

                    ARCHIE GALBONI (CASNIO OWNER LEADER)
               (hands-up over
                face, begging for
                mercy)
          --L--Listen! I'll give you
          whatever you want, alright?
          Just--Just let me live. Tell
          TECH--tell 'em, he can have the
          CASINOS, all of 'em!!! But, I
          can't die tonight, please, don't
          do this!!!

                    MIA MAELSTROM
               (lifts her sword
                as to strike)
          --You pitiful, pathetic
          parasite.--

MIA MAELSTROM slices ARCHIE GALBONI to bits and pieces...

                    MIA MAELSTROM
               (into her
                comms-device)
          --Mi Amor, IT IS FINISHED.--

                    TECH THE TYRANT
               (through MIA's
                comms-device)
          --Good, return to me...Good work,
          MIA. When you get here, you and I
          are going to pay a visit to one of
          my fighters, a DR. VEGAS. He
          killed my crew on the job, even
          our BODYGUARD. And, he took a ton
          of our cash after doing so.--

                    MIA MAELSTROM
          --I will make him wish he'd never
          existed, baby...

                                        CUT TO:

EXT. THE LAS VEGAS STRIP - NIGHT

                                   YEAR: 2013

A young MIA MAELSTROM walks the strip.

She is a tourist, with a couple of girlfriends, simply having a good-time.

                    GIRLFRIEND 1
          --We're definitely finding a guy
          tonight, and we're going to run
          the train on 'em.--

                    GIRLFRIEND 2
          --You slut-bucket. That does sound
          enticing though. MIA? What'd you
          think?

                    MIA MAELSTROM
          --I'd fuck a pillow right now if I
          could.

The three lovely women walk up to a CASINO; the MGM GRAND.

                    GIRLFRIEND 1
          --We've got, what? 2 grand left,
          between the three of us?

                    MIA MAELSTROM
          Yeah, something like that. Give or
          take.

                    GIRLFRIEND 2
          --I'm goin' in this CASINO. You
          guys are comin' with me. We're
          gonna gamble a bit, then, I just
          know, we'll find our trick or
          tricks, re-up and repeat till next
          Thursday. Can't beat it.

                    MIA MAELSTROM
          --You two go ahead of me. I'm
          sneaking a few tokes before I go
          in there.

                    GIRLFRIEND 1
          --You're a pot-head, hoe.

                    MIA MAELSTROM
                 (gives the middle
                  finger to her
                  girlfriends)
          --Ah, you cunt-scabs. I'll be
          right in, no worries.--

MIA's girlfriends enter the CASINO without her.

She walks to the side a bit in the glimmer of darkness next

to a bulky-column. MIA retrieves her "Dug-Out", a
wooden-device that holds marijuana, she then pulls out her
"bat", a metal pipe-contraption that resembles a cigarette,
and allows pot to be packed and smoked easily in public
without too much suspicion.

> MIA MAELSTROM
> (puffs her
> pinch-hitter)
> --The City of Sin. I might never
> leave he---

> TECH THE TYRANT
> (grabs MIA from
> behind)
> --Sleep.--

The young woman struggles to free herself, only to fail.

TECH has disabled her with chloroform.

She's out. He drags her to a town-car, throws her in the
back, and his driver takes TECH and MIA MAELSTROM off. She
has been kidnapped. This is how they met.

> CUT TO:

INT. TORTURE-CHAMBER - LATER

MIA wakes up, completely subdued and restrained.

Scared stiff.

TECH enters the TORTURE CHAMBER as she awakens.

> MIA MAELSTROM
> (fighting the
> restraints)
> --Who--Who are You? Why am I here?
> Where are my girls?!!! Goddammit
> let me out of here!!!

MIA is shocked by TECH's appearance. The metal arms,
red-eyes. He's a intimidating person to look at it. More
machine than man, from her perspective.

> TECH THE TYRANT
> --My sweet, after I'm through with
> you, you'll be a monster like me.
> You'll serve my will, and only
> that. I've been observing you Ms.
> Maelstrom, since you arrived in my
> town, and I must say, you have
> (MORE)

                         TECH THE TYRANT (cont'd)
          great potential. Now, let's start
          the pain.--

TECH grabs MIA by the throat, after taking off her
restraints. He then drags her to the other side of the
TORTURE CHAMBER, there is a 'IRON-MAIDEN'-trap on that side
of the place.

The IRON-MAIDEN device is open, needles are all on the
inside of the ancient-torture-mechanism.

                         MIA MAELSTROM
          --NO! Please, Don't Do This!!!

                         TECH THE TYRANT
          --This is not my doing...FATE HAS
          CHOSEN YOU.

TECH throws MIA inside the IRON-MAIDEN, and slams it shut.
The needles within the machine pierce her soft-flesh.

                         MIA MAELSTROM
                    (screaming at the
                     top-of-her-lungs)
          AaHHH!!!

TECH stands near the IRON-MAIDEN after sealing his kidnapped
victim in it. Her blood drains and runs off through
vein-like contraptions connected to the floor; TECH catches
the blood as it runs, into a golden-goblet. He fills it to
the brim, and lets the rest waste...

He loves the sound of her screams. He smiles with such
poisonous charm at the sound of the wailing from MIA as he
drinks her blood from his gold-goblet.

                         TECH THE TYRANT
                    (smiling from
                     ear-to-ear)
          --THERE'S POWER IN THE BLOOD--

                                             CUT TO:

INT. THE WAITING ROOM - DAY

The news is on the TV in VEGAS' waiting room.

                         NEWS-ANCHOR
                    (on the television)
          --Chaos was unleashed last night
          in Los Angeles. Death took too
          many, the numbers haven't stopped.
                         (MORE)

                         NEWS-ANCHOR (cont'd)
          The military was hacked last
          night, and its drones with it.
          Those unmanned aircraft were used
          to attack the greater city of LA.
          The structural damage is
          catastrophic, the death toll
          cataclysmic. I'm being told that
          the Pentagon has no earthly idea
          who, or what hacked their systems
          and caused this terror attack. We
          will update you as the sources
          provide more information. Thank
          you.---
                    (signs off)

                         PATIENT 2
          --Fucking Muslims...

                         PATIENT 3
          --Now, that's jumpin' to
          conclusions don't ya think? How
          the hell a bunch of cave-monkeys
          gonna perform a cyber-attack on
          American-Soil? Answer me that,
          asshole. Hell, I'm more worried
          about the homos than I am the
          Jihadists...

                                        CUT TO:

INT. DR. VEGAS' OFFICE - CONTINUOUS

PATIENTs are entering and exiting THE BACK POPPING ROOM
consistently. DR. VEGAS is getting his work-done.

The money, 180K, is stashed in his safe, in the back of his
OFFICE in the same case VEGAS found it in.

                         DR. ALEXANDER VEGAS
                    (talking to a
                     leaving patient)
          --Alrighty, you have a good day as
          well, madam.--Okay, now--MAYA CO--

BULLETS RIDDLE THROUGH THE GLASS-DOOR, AND THE OFFICE
ITSELF. All 5 Patients in the building die randomly.

SARAH THE SECRETARY is struck with a flesh wound.

MRS. BRETSKI is also hit, in the leg.

VEGAS runs to SARAH and BRETSKI's aid and gets them to safety, dodging the hot-bullets.

                    SARAH THE SECRETARY
                 (screaming)
            Aah!!!

                    MS. BRETSKI
                 (going into shock)
            We--we're so fucked...

                    DR. ALEXANDER VEGAS
            --Come on, guys, into the back.
            NOW!

VEGAS, practically carrying both of his ladies, exits through the back of the OFFICE.

                                        CUT TO:

EXT. VEGAS' OFFICE - CONTINUOUS

DR. VEGAS exits with SARAH and MRS. BRETSKI only to be surrounded by TECH THE TYRANT himself, along with MIA MAELSTROM and 4 other SHOOTERS with their weapons, with laser-sights, pointed at VEGAS and his ladies.

                    TECH THE TYRANT
                 (smirking)
            --Wow, the great prize-fighter of
            THE UNDERWORLD. DR. VEGAS...you
            know, I own the majority of THE
            UNDERWORLD. I have more stake than
            any of the other share-holders.
            So, by technicality, my Good
            Doctor; YOU ARE MY PROPERTY. You
            owe me a fight. But, I don't want
            that. I want my Goddamn Money
            right now, or I'm torturing these
            women here...if you give me the
            money, I'm just gonna take you,
            agreed?

VEGAS stumbles, he pauses...

                    MS. BRETSKI
            What money is he--what's he
            talking about, ALEX?

                    SARAH THE SECRETARY
                  (consumed by fear)
        --Give it to 'em, please,
        DOCTOR!!!

                    MIA MAELSTROM
        --Sir, if you don't provide TECH's
        cash back to him, I WILL CUT YOUR
        HEAD OFF...then he will feast on
        your headless corpse.--

                    DR. ALEXANDER VEGAS
        9211991...
                  (shamed)
        ---It's in the safe, in the
        back...

                    TECH THE TYRANT
                  (satisfied)
        --Now, see, you can right your
        wrongs in this World...
                  (to his SHOOTERS)
        Bag him, boys. Leave the women be.
        They've done no wrong.

The SHOOTERS all say: "Yes, Boss." in Harmony.

They restrain VEGAS and put a black-bag over his head.

He doesn't fight back as they put him in TECH's HUMMER.

                    MS. BRETSKI
        --Where are you taking him?!--

                    TECH THE TYRANT
        --To the other side, Ma'am...

TECH walks into the OFFICE himself. He's going to retrieve
the cash.

He does so collected, composed.

                    SARAH THE SECRETARY
                  (gets up to fight
                   the SHOOTERS and
                   help VEGAS)
        --NO!!!

                    DR. ALEXANDER VEGAS
                  (inside the
                   HUMMER, hearing
                   the noise)
        --Sarah! Don't!--

MIA MAELSTROM punches SARAH so hard that she flies back about 7 ft. It knocks the breath out of her, and she struggles to regain it. But, it wasn't a lethal blow, just a warning shot...

                              CUT TO:

INT. VEGAS' OFFICE - MOMENTS LATER

TECH puts in the code that VEGAS gave him.

The safe opens.

                    TECH THE TYRANT
                (looks at the
                 money, counts it)
              --Cash Rules Everything Around
            Me.--

TECH digs deep into the case of cash.

He pulls a tracking device, a RFID-Chip, that was laced into one of the bills, out of the case. He crushes the Radio-Frequency-Identification device.

                              CUT TO:

EXT. VEGAS' OFFICE - MOMENTS LATER

TECH exits with the money in-hand.

He, MIA, the SHOOTERS leave the scene of CHAOS with DR. VEGAS in their possession.

                              CUT TO:

INT. TECH'S MANSION - NIGHT

TECH rarely enters his living-room, but on this occasion he has. MIA MAELSTROM sits to the side in a luxurious chair, polishing her samurai steel.

DR. VEGAS is tied and bound to TECH's pool table. He's tied with rope, and plenty of knots.

                    DR. ALEXANDER VEGAS
              --So, you're TECH--THE TYRANT?

                    TECH THE TYRANT
          --You've heard of me, I'm
          flattered my Good Doctor.
          Flattered very much indeed. We
          have many words to exchange till
          you meet your death. But, I'm no
          'BOND'-villain. No. Your head will
          be on my desk in, ah, the next
          hour. In a glass case, if you were
          wondering. Your brain and some of
          your other organs will be consumed
          by me personally, fried,
          like--chicken--. Makes my mouth
          water thinkin' about it.

                    DR. ALEXANDER VEGAS
          You're the madman trying to
          takeover MY CITY, huh?

                    TECH THE TYRANT
          I'm no Man...no, I'm far beyond
          that, Doc. And, yeah, this is MY
          CITY. I have the signatures of the
          dead CASINO bosses to prove it.
          Tomorrow, mid-day, there will be
          CHAOTIC-demolitions. All the
          casinos will fall, with all the
          petty gamblers inside. Then, I
          will helm the reconstruction of
          the city. All the major Casinos
          will be consolidated into my very
          own. Yes, VEGAS is mine indeed.

                    DR. ALEXANDER VEGAS
          --Delusions of grandiosity,
          nothing an ass-whoopin couldn't
          cure for ya.

                    TECH THE TYRANT
          Fighting is so--boring, barbaric.
          Torture on the other hand? It's
          PLEASURE...MIA, please, let's go
          to work on our friend here.

TECH walks up to DR. VEGAS devastates him with two punches
to the face. TECH's cold metallic arms hurt him more than
he's ever been by jabs.

MIA gets up and walks to the pool table, sword in hand,
ready...

                         MIA MAELSTROM
                    --You're gonna feel a little
                    pressure, DOCTOR.

She cuts VEGAS' shirt in half down his torso, revealing his
fit upper-body. Her sword cuts the shirt like butter, it's
that sharp...

VEGAS shakes and stirs, attempting to break free to no
avail.

                         TECH THE TYRANT
                    YOU CANNOT FIGHT DEATH, Dr. Vegas.

After uttering this sentence, gun-fire can be heard outside
of TECH's MANSION.

The gun-fire gets closer. TECH backs up...

MIA readies herself, and goes up to the door.

She puts her ear up to the door, and out-of-nowhere a blast
occurs, knocking her back several feet.

A shadow, a shape enters with a automatic weapon in-hand.

                         MR. ROYCE
                    --Now, I got two weapons on my
                    person...my prosthetic leg, and my
                    automatic rifle. AND, I AIN'T
                    USING THE LEG!

RAYMOND ROYCE, after making his grand-entrance, sprays away
at TECH and MIA, both of whom hide behind furniture in the
open-spaced area to avoid gun-fire from the former vet.

ROYCE quits shooting for a moment.

He hobbles up to DR. VEGAS and cuts him loose off the table.

                         DR. ALEXANDER VEGAS
                         (in disbelief)
                    What are you doing here, sir?

                         MR. ROYCE
                    --SAVING YOUR ASS, SOLDIER!--

VEGAS gets up, and he and ROYCE start to exit, but are
stopped by MIA's blade, which she throws at the wall near
their heads, piercing it like a piece of paper.

                    MIA MAELSTROM
               (points her finger
                at them)
          --YOU TWO AREN'T LEAVING HERE
          ALIVE...

VEGAS gestures to ROYCE to go to the side. He does.

                    DR. ALEXANDER VEGAS
               (to MIA)
          --You little cunt, I'll fight you
          just like I would any man.

                    MIA MAELSTROM
          --TECH, leave. I'll handle this.

                    TECH THE TYRANT
          --But, my love?--What if--

                    MIA MAELSTROM
          --Just do it.--

TECH hastily exits the living-room through a safe-door to an
unknown area.

MIA MAELSTROM reaches her hand out, and with a magnetic-like
technological device, wrapped around the wrist, that sparks,
pulls her sword from out of the wall back to her hand...the
swords land in her hand, and she charges VEGAS...

                                        CUT TO:

ROYCE reloads his weapon quickly, and shoots at MIA...

She slices all the bullets with her sword. She's that fast.

ROYCE is shocked.

                    DR. ALEXANDER VEGAS
               MR. ROYCE, cease-fire...

                    MIA MAELSTROM
          --You have no earthly idea who
          you're going up against, do you,
          DR. VEGAS? I'm no
          cage-fighter--with this sword, I'm
          the deadliest person you'll ever
          encounter...now, let's tango.

                    DR. ALEXANDER VEGAS
          --Yes, Ma'am.--

MIA lunges at VEGAS, slices his stomach immediately, not
fatally though.

> DR. ALEXANDER VEGAS
> (stomach bleeding)
> --Holy Fuck!--

MIA tries to cut VEGAS several more times, he luckily dodges
her strikes, with great difficulty.

However, Ms. MAELSTROM then cuts VEGAS' hand, and lacerates
his face...

> MIA MAELSTROM
> --Your eyes are purple...yet, you
> bleed red like all men. You're
> nothing special, VEGAS. Just
> another man to taste my deathly
> blade.--

> DR. ALEXANDER VEGAS
> --You're like all women, you talk
> too fuckin' much...

MIA MAELSTROM goes to attack DR. VEGAS with a terrifying
stroke, downward toward the top of his skull.

> MIA MAELSTROM
> (with full force)
> --AAH!!!

VEGAS stops the blade with his hands before it hits him.

He and MIA then struggle...

VEGAS distracts MIA for a split-second, moves the other way
and manages to flip the sword in the air for a moment.

DR. VEGAS, as MIA looks up to her sword, KICKS HER SQUARE IN
THE VAGINA. This low-blow devastates her.

She falls to her knees.

VEGAS retrieves the sword, and places it at MIA's head.

> MIA MAELSTROM
> --I never wanted to die a
> monster...

> DR. ALEXANDER VEGAS
> You fucked with the wrong
> doctor...

DR. VEGAS cuts MIA's head off, then and there. NO MERCY. It rolls around on the ground for a second, but then comes to a dead-stop. Her facial expression is one of pain and fear.

                    MR. ROYCE
                (appears out from
                 his cover)
        --That bitch had it comin'. Good
        work, VEGAS. Now, let's get the
        fuck out of this mad-house.

VEGAS falls to the floor.

ROYCE picks him up off of his feet.

They proceed to exit the MANSION.

There are none to contest the two; ROYCE killed 'em all...

                              CUT TO:

EXT. THE FRONT YARD - MOMENTS LATER

VEGAS, being held up by ROYCE, evades through the FRONT-YARD of TECH's property.

They are contested on the spot, by TECH THE TYRANT himself.

He is about 20 feet away, having appeared from out of nowhere.

                    TECH THE TYRANT
        VEGAS! STOP!--Where--WHERE IS MIA?

                    DR. ALEXANDER VEGAS
        --Dead as a door-nail in your
        humble-abode.

                    TECH THE TYRANT
                (shakes his head,
                 gets teary-eyed)
        --She was CHAOS--IN THE FLESH--you
        killed the purest being I've ever
        encountered...SHE WAS THE ONLY
        THING THAT EVER LOVED ME. Now, you
        will meet Death yourself. You and
        your ally here.

                    MR. ROYCE
        --Metal Arms? Red-Eyes? What are
        you, man? A Terminator?---

                    DR. ALEXANDER VEGAS
              --Shoot the bastard.---

ROYCE goes to fire, 7 bullets are shot at TECH and he blocks
them with his metal arms...

His red-eyes intensify, he charges ROYCE and VEGAS.

TECH disarms ROYCE within a split-moment. TECH breaks the
automatic weapon into pieces---his metal arms give him the
strength of 4 men.

TECH bitch-slaps VEGAS, he falls back and slides in the
grass a few feet.

THE TYRANT picks up ROYCE by the neck...almost crushing his
spine...

                    TECH THE TYRANT
                 (mad as a bull
                  seeing red)
              Aah!!!

VEGAS gets up quickly, and races to save ROYCE.

He tackles TECH so hard that TECH lets go of ROYCE. ROYCE
backs away and falls on his back, almost unconscious.

VEGAS and TECH get up at the same time, and square up to
fight.

                    DR. ALEXANDER VEGAS
              --Fight me, you piece of shit,
              leave the old man out of this.

                    TECH THE TYRANT
              --To the Death, Doctor, no
              holds-barred, no bets...you got
              it.

TECH jukes toward VEGAS like a jaguar, and hits him with a
right-hook that would hurt The Devil himself.

VEGAS is already injured pretty roughly.

TECH hits VEGAS with a uppercut, and three left jabs.

THE TYRANT kicks VEGAS in the stomach.

                    TECH THE TYRANT
              --Why do you think I invented the
              UNDERWORLD FIGHTING for OUR CITY?
              I did it, because I myself enjoy
              the martial arts...now, fight me,
                      (MORE)

                    TECH THE TYRANT (cont'd)
        DOCTOR.

VEGAS gets up, and he attacks TECH with all he has.

DR. VEGAS swings a few times and misses, TECH capitalizes
with a couple hooks. He goes to throw a third, and DR. VEGAS
stops his punch mid-way.

                    DR. ALEXANDER VEGAS
            --I know your next move.--

VEGAS wraps his arm around the metal arm of TECH.

He does so with the other arm, trapping the tyrant.

VEGAS head-buts TECH three times, hurting the madman...

VEGAS lets go of the tyrant, only to run back up to him and
knee him in the face. The good doctor then, rapidly, punches
and kicks TECH several times.

TECH backs up, and takes a knee, out of breath, hurt.

VEGAS stands tall against THE TYRANT.

                    TECH THE TYRANT
            --Doc--I DO NOT FIGHT FAIR...

TECH pulls a 9MM Pistol, and shoots VEGAS in his right
shoulder. VEGAS falls back.

TECH gets up and walks toward VEGAS to finish him off.

Out-of-the-blue, MR. ROYCE comes to VEGAS' aid..

He hits THE TYRANT on the head with his prosthetic leg, the
metal part. It incapacitates TECH.

While TECH's down, ROYCE re-attaches his leg and goes to
check on DR. VEGAS.

                    MR. ROYCE
                (examines the
                 gun-shot wound)
            --Ah, you'll be okay. Get up, ya
            pussy.--It's through-and-through,
            didn't hit any vitals.--
                (extends his hand
                 to VEGAS)
            --Now, get up, soldier.

ROYCE picks VEGAS up; the doctor stands.

He regathers himself, and then approaches the downed TECH.

DR. VEGAS punches TECH three times in the face, then rolls
him over onto his stomach.

              TECH THE TYRANT
       What are you doing, motherfucker?!

             DR. ALEXANDER VEGAS
     --YOUR SPINE NEEDS ADJUSTING...

Dr. Vegas, with all his strength, penetrates TECH's
back-area, and rips out his spine with the skull attached.

He looks at the bloody mess, and throws the spine to the
ground, beside the lifeless TECH THE TYRANT...

ROYCE and VEGAS start to leave TECH's property.

              MR. ROYCE
     --You must've watched a lot of
     'Predator', huh?

             DR. ALEXANDER VEGAS
     --It's in my top-10 films...so,
     yeah.

VEGAS grunts in great pain...

              MR. ROYCE
     --You okay, son?

             DR. ALEXANDER VEGAS
     --I'll make it.--I'm just ready to
     get back to work. How'd you find
     me, sir?

              MR. ROYCE
     --You're in no condition to work.
     We need to get you first-aid,
     asap. And, I found you, because
     I'm CIA. It's what I do. Been on
     TECH's trail for some time, but
     I've not had clearance to do
     anything about him. And--Doc--I'm
     not just a random patient of
     yours...I AM YOUR FATHER.

             DR. ALEXANDER VEGAS
     --What the fuc---

DR. VEGAS has fought the good fight; saving the Sin City from tremendous Tyranny...all with his long-lost father's assistance...

                              CUT TO BLACK:

ACT III. DUALITY

                              FADE IN:

                              LOCATION: PANAMA
                              CITY, FLORIDA

YEAR: 1991

EXT. NEIGHBORHOOD/THE CORTEZ RESIDENCE - AFTERNOON

In a random neighborhood in PANAMA CITY, FLORIDA, a BUS filled with excited, gleeful children pulls up to a home and stops.

Two young girls, 9 and 10 years of age, exit the bus, they are sisters. They walk up to the front door of their home.

The door is slightly cracked...

They enter reluctantly.

                              CUT TO:

INT. THE CORTEZ RESIDENCE - CONTINUOUS

The girls walk in to a bloody sight. Blood is on the floor, on the walls of the 3 bedroom, 2 bathroom home.

The girls, however, do not tuck-tail. No. They go further into the silent home.

The silence quickly evaporates, as their mother's painful screams can be heard, along with two voices.

                    GIRL 1
               (fearful of the
                screams)
          --Mama!?--

                    GIRL 2
          --HE'S BEATING HER AGAIN...what
          are we gonna do? He'll probably
          TOUCH us after he's through...

154

                    GIRL 1
          --We're not sitting back this
          time. We're going to do something,
          that's what.

                    GIRL 2
          I'll get us a knife.

The girls both equip themselves with a kitchen-knife.

They then move toward the noises.

The bathroom is where they're coming from.

                              CUT TO:

INT. THE CORTEZ RESIDENCE/THE HALLWAY - MOMENTS LATER

The girls see a WOMAN, the ADULTRESS, sitting atop their
MOTHER, punching her, over and over, all while their
Step-Dad, SERGIO CORTEZ, holds her arms and head down...

The girls react...they charge their Step-Father and his
mistress.

                    GIRL 1
          --Leave Her Alone!!!--

                    SERGIO CORTEZ
             (gets up to strike
              GIRL 2)
          --You Little Bitches are
          Next!!!---

                    ADULTRESS
          --Get 'em now, SERGIO, I'll take
          care of this bitch.

                    GIRL 2
             (with the knife
              in-hand)
          --Aah!!!---

GIRL 1 jumps at SERGIO, and stabs him in the side of the
neck.

Blood splatters everywhere.

SERGIO kneels and holds his wounded neck, but he's not
dying.

GIRL 2 runs up behind the ADULTRESS, who's still punching her Mom, and like a damn ninja she slits the ADULTRESSES throat from behind.

Their bloodied and beaten Mom gets up and runs to the bedroom, grabs a pistol out of the dresser...

                    ANGELA CORTEZ
                 (to SERGIO, gun
                  pointed at him)
            --Feel this, you fucking
            piece-of-shit!!!

ANGELA CORTEZ grabs her daughters and shields them from the horror taking place.

The hurt mother, protecting her daughters, fires five-bullets into SERGIO.

The Adultress is already dead, but ANGELA still fires a bullet right between-her-eyes.

The revolver is empty.

ANGELA turns herself and children from the sight of death, and she falls in her own tears...her daughters hug her after dropping their knives.

A noise is heard near the front of the house.

                                        CUT TO:

A COP, MARTIN MALICE, is responding to the call after the gun-fire.

He sees the GIRLS and their MOTHER, as well as the 2 dead bodies.

He does what he's trained to do, as the mother points the empty pistol at the OFFICER.

                    ANGELA CORTEZ
                 (pointing the
                  revolver at the
                  OFFICER)
            --Stay away from my children.--

                 DETECTIVE MARTIN MALICE
            --Drop the weapon, now!!! OR I
            WILL SHOOT!!!

                    GIRL 1
            --Please, don't shoot, it's EM---

Before the GIRL can finish her sentence, the OFFICER fires three rounds into ANGELA CORTEZ. Two in the chest, one in the head; killing her on the spot.

> GIRL 1
> (yelling with her
> sister,
> Frantically)
> --NO!!!---

> DETECTIVE MARTIN MALICE
> (into his radio)
> --This is MALICE. I need EMT, I need back-up now at 223 GULF VIEW. I have three dead. I also have 2 children that need social-services and psychological evaluation.

> DISPATCH
> --Your Responders are nearing, MALICE. Sit tight.

The OFFICER rubs his hands through his hair, realizing the gravity of what he's done; ripping a mother from her children.

He tries to appeal to the young GIRLS with no success, they refuse to leave their mother.

> DETECTIVE MARTIN MALICE
> --It's okay, you guys. I'm a Cop. I won't hurt you, I promise. Just please leave this bathroom. This is not good for you to be in here. Maybe you can tell me all that happened. Help will be here soon. Please, step away from the bodies...

The GIRLS both give him a "death-stare"...

> GIRL 1
> --You will not get away with this...

> GIRL 2
> Death will have it's day for you, too, MALICE...now, WAKE UP!!!

The man is stunned by the child's statement. He falls back into a darkly-abyss...

                    DETECTIVE MARTIN MALICE
              (falling)
          --Aah!!!

                                        CUT TO:

INT. POLICE-VEHICLE - EVENING

                                   YEAR: 2018

DETECTIVE MARTIN MALICE wakes up frightened.

He starts his car and drives off speedily...

He's supposed to be at a crime-scene, but had to park a
couple of miles away from it, because he's drunk.

The massive-murder scene is in the woods of WEWAHITCHKA, at
the estate of CAPTAIN KARL NOOSE...

                    DETECTIVE MARTIN MALICE
              (narrating,
               driving)
          ---I am drowning in my own tears.
          Alcohol isn't habit-forming...I
          should know, been using it for
          decades. I sincerely can't wait to
          be out of this shit. Anything goes
          wrong, they call me, like I'm the
          fucking 'Ghost-Busters'. The head
          of the KKK gets whacked and these
          WEWA fuckheads want my expertise.
          Some guy named: CAPTAIN NOOSE.
          Sounds like I'm in a fucking
          comic-book...I smell like
          booze...been drinking since 4 AM.
          I am as far from sober as the
          heavens are from earth...They
          won't notice. Even if they do, my
          badge supersedes...I know how
          this'll go. I'll look at the dead
          body for 15 minutes, and get told
          a summary of the events, the name
          of the suspect, and I'll be told
          to find 'em. And, I won't. Not
          because I can't, but because I
          don't give two-fucks. Being a cop
          is the only thing I know how to
          do, but I question the
          law...MYSELF, incessantly. I wanna
          give up, but I need my pension.
          I'll probably lose my mind before
          I get it. It doesn't matter. When
                    (MORE)

                    DETECTIVE MARTIN MALICE (cont'd)
          I lost my Wife, I lost everything.
          The cancer ate her up. I had to
          watch her for 102 days, die
          slowly. Death is a peeping
          Tom--but, it don't faze me.
          Neither does killin'. I have
          killed before. I still see all
          their faces...in my dreams. We are
          not hypocrites in our sleep.---The
          Alcohol...it just makes the
          nightmares worse, but hell, if I
          don't drink, I shake so bad I
          can't drive. First I take a drink,
          then the drink takes a drink, then
          the drink takes me. But, hell,
          there are more old-drunkards than
          there are old-doctors, so my luck
          may prevail, even if my health
          fails.---I'm so sick of this. Fuck
          duty. The call needs to be
          answered by someone else.---My
          therapist thinks I'm having a
          second mid-life crisis. The
          therapy helps, to some degree or
          another, but, my head is still
          fucked up from this job. I like
          the therapist. She's a beautiful
          woman, kind, and friendly; I've
          opened up to her in ways I've
          never done with anybody, even
          SUSAN. They put me in therapy to
          get me straight, but, my pain,
          it's endless. Not too much longer,
          and I'll be done with all this
          bullshit.--

MARTIN MALICE pulls up to the crime-scene in the rural
KKK-infested area.

He exits his vehicle, and proceeds over to the other
authorities.

EXT. CRIME-SCENE/THE NOOSE ESTATE - CONTINUOUS

MALICE walks cautiously over to a WASTEPRO TRUCK.

He looks about the same as he did in '91.

He's a small-man. 5'9, 173 pounds. He has short black hair,
and has stubble all over his face. Hazel eyes. He's 55 years
old, yet still handsome, in a George Clooney kind of way.

FORENSIC INVESTIGATORS are all over, taking pictures, gathering clues.

The Garbage Truck reeks of not just trash, but of rotting human-flesh...

                    DETECTIVE MARTIN MALICE
                (disturbed by the
                 scene)
          Fuck a Duck.
                (to FORENSIC
                 INVESTIGATOR 1)
          --What the hell am I lookin' at?

The FORENSIC INVESTIGATOR is no older than 25...a young guy.

                    FORENSIC INVESTIGATOR 1
                (walking around
                 taking photos)
          --Well, our suspect, a TRICKEY
          BREEDLOVE, killed several
          KKK-Members, we've stacked and
          packed their bodies. But, the
          maniacal son-of-a-gun killed the
          LEADER of THE KKK by throwin' 'em
          in this here truck, and smashing
          him in the hopper with the
          compactor. Talk about a Death for
          the Ages...

                    DETECTIVE MARTIN MALICE
          --I'll be damned. Who's this
          TRICKEY BREEDLOVE-fella? Any
          sufficient leads on him yet?

                    FORENSIC INVESTIGATOR 1
          --No, sir, none at all. No
          sightings, no nothing. I hear the
          guy is ex-military, dishonorable,
          so we may be dealing with a
          psychopath.

                    DETECTIVE MARTIN MALICE
                (examining the
                 mushed up corpse
                 of CAPTAIN NOOSE)
          --If you ask me, I say
          good-riddance...hell, THE KKK are
          a bunch of terrorists. You and I
          both know that they were trying to
          kill that man, and somehow FATE
          itself allowed him to kill all
                    (MORE)

                    DETECTIVE MARTIN MALICE (cont'd)
          these assholes.

                    FORENSIC INVESTIGATOR 1
          --That's not your job, to say
          who's right or wrong. Good or bad.
          Your job is to find the
          perpetrator of this CHAOS,
          DETECTIVE. Men died here, right or
          wrong, there are consequences for
          that type of behavior.

                    DETECTIVE MARTIN MALICE
                    (lights a
                     cigarette)
          --You know what---fuck you and the
          horse you rode in on, man. I
          didn't come here to be lectured by
          a millennial. I'm fuckin' out of
          here.

Puffing his cigarette, he starts to leave the scene cool
like the Fonz.

He gets into his vehicle after the more than futile trip,
and takes off back to PANAMA CITY.

                    CUT TO:

INT. PANAMA CITY SPIRITS STORE - NIGHT

After making the 1 hour trip back to PC, MALICE has entered
a SPIRITS STORE.

He makes his selection, same one he always makes: 'JOSE
CUERVO' TEQUILA

TEQUILA keeps him up, so he isn't too drunk on the job.

                    LIQUOR STORE CLERK
          --That'll be 23.85, sir.--

                    DETECTIVE MARTIN MALICE
          Alright, how ya' doin' tonight,
          miss? I've never seen you in here
          before.

                    LIQUOR STORE CLERK
          --I'm well, thank you. How about
          yourself?--And, yeah, I just
          started yesterday.

MARTIN is far older than this female LIQUOR STORE CLERK.

However, he still makes a move.

                    DETECTIVE MARTIN MALICE
          --I'm Good. I'd be doing better if
          you'd come and drink with me,
          let's say, when you get off???--

                    LIQUOR STORE CLERK
                    (patronizing)
          --Get Lost, Creep.

                    DETECTIVE MARTIN MALICE
                    (persistent)
          --I just--I just would like to
          have someone to spend the night
          with me, is all, miss, I---

                    LIQUOR STORE CLERK
          --I'm callin' the cops, now.---

                    DETECTIVE MARTIN MALICE
                    (reveals his badge)
          --I AM THE COPS, Honey. Here's 50
          Bucks, keep the change, you
          little-cunt...

MALICE throws a 50 at the CLERK.

She is unsettled and on-the-edge.

The DETECTIVE exits, in a stupefied rage.

                                        CUT TO:

INT. MALICE'S HOME - LATER

MALICE enters his HOME with his LIQUOR.

He's already drank half of the bottle.

He stumbles in, and slams the door. MALICE takes two more
huge sips, and he falls flat on his face, pukes, and lies in
his own vomit...

THE DETECTIVE ENTERS A DREAM STATE...

                                        CUT TO:

INT. DREAM SEQUENCE - CONTINUOUS

MARTIN MALICE wakes up in a HOSPITAL.

His WIFE is screaming his name. He can hear her screams down the black-hallway, shrouded in darkness.

> MARTIN'S WIFE
> --MARTIN!!! HELP ME!!! I--I CAN'T
> BREATHE!!!

> DETECTIVE MARTIN MALICE
> (sprinting toward
> the sound of her
> pain)
> --SUSAN!? Susan! Where are You?

As MARTIN runs through the blackness, light shines ahead of him. He can see.

A person is at the end of the hallway, standing still as a statue.

MARTIN MALICE stops in his tracks, and sees that the person is NOT his WIFE.

He's never seen this woman before...

> VICTIM 1
> (naked and
> shivering)
> --Why?--Why have YOU let this
> happen?--

The WOMAN, VICTIM 1, starts bleeding from her eyes. Her breasts fall off of her body...blood starts flowing from all of her body entries.

The blood begins to build-up, and flood, it goes like a wave toward MARTIN MALICE.

MARTIN runs back the other way.

> DETECTIVE MARTIN MALICE
> (running as fast
> as he can)
> Aah!!!

The Detective's legs sink into the floor. His feet are cemented to it.

He's stuck like chuck. The BLOOD FLOWS all around Him, and consumes Him. He suffocates with pure agony...

CUT TO:

INT. MARTIN'S HOME - MORNING

MR. MALICE snaps out of his nightmarish vision.

He gets up out of his vomit, opens his TEQUILA and chugs the remainder like it's a bottle of water.

The DETECTIVE showers, dresses, gathers his belongings, and leaves to start the new day.

Before he exits, he stares into the mirror.

                    DETECTIVE MARTIN MALICE
                (into the mirror)
            --It wasn't your fault. You had to
            do it.---It was Me or Her...

He exits his HOME...

                                        CUT TO:

INT. POLICE-CRUISER - MOMENTS LATER

While cruising to THE POLICE DEPARTMENT, MALICE receives a phone-call...from THE CHIEF.

                    DETECTIVE MARTIN MALICE
                (talking into his
                 phone)
            Hello?

                    THE CHIEF
                (through the phone)
            --MALICE, you never answer your
            goddamn phone! I've called you at
            least 25 fucking times in the last
            3 hours! What the fuck!?

                    DETECTIVE MARTIN MALICE
            --Fuck the What?--

                    THE CHIEF
            --Don't you get smart with me, you
            son-of-a-bitch! Now--you gotta a
            new partner coming in today. A
            woman. You're gonna show her the
            ropes for the next two months,
            then she'll be on her own like
            you. When you retire next year,
                    (MORE)

                    THE CHIEF (cont'd)
she'll be your replacement.

                    DETECTIVE MARTIN MALICE
--But, CHIEF---

                    THE CHIEF
MALICE, come on, man, I don't
wanna hear it, alright. Get here
now, so you can meet ANGEL, and so
I can brief you two. A corpse was
found in an abandoned house on
BASS STREET; ANGEL is going with
you on any-and-all of your new
cases. No backtalk either.--

                    DETECTIVE MARTIN MALICE
--Whatever, Prick.--

                    THE CHIEF
--You Son-of-a---

MALICE hangs up the phone with urgency.

                                        CUT TO:

EXT. PANAMA CITY - CONTINUOUS

Scum and villainy are all-over in PANAMA CITY. It's
ostensibly nice, but underneath--underneath it is wretched
and crime-ridden. Drugs, Gambling, Prostitution,
Racketeering, Robbery, you name it, it happens here...just
like any other city, really.

MALICE is neither for, nor against the CHAOS. He stays so
drunk, that the bottles drink from Him...

                    DETECTIVE MARTIN MALICE
                         (narrating)
                    --My Life is Hell. Hell is the
                    place where THE WORM DIETH NOT AND
                    THE FIRE IS NEVER QUENCHED. On
                    this earth, I'm just awaiting
                    Death. With Susan gone, everything
                    is without purpose for me. Nothing
                    means anything to me anymore.
                    Sometimes I wear the ring, around
                    the house; just to feel some
                    semblance that she is there...or
                    was there. She--she is always in
                    my dreams and nightmares. I wake
                    up, and it's still a nightmare. My
                    dreams---they feel real when I'm
                              (MORE)

>   DETECTIVE MARTIN MALICE (cont'd)
>   in them, and this reality, when
>   I'm awake--feels more and more
>   distant. More and more out of
>   reach. I'm sinking into the depths
>   of HELL and I know it. FATE is
>   calling me there...

MALICE drives faster, rushing to get the day done so he can down more of the snake-that-bit-him.

                                        CUT TO:

INT. THE POLICE-STATION - LATER

MARTIN MALICE walks through the STATION, only to be looked down upon by his colleagues and even his lowers, they give the look of disdain, contempt...because, he's a drunk and because he's an asshole.

He goes straight to the CHIEF's OFFICE, to meet his new partner/trainee.

                                        CUT TO:

INT. THE CHIEF'S OFFICE - MOMENTS LATER

>   THE CHIEF
>   (mid-discussion)
>   --There was a news report of a guy
>   driving on the wrong side of the
>   highway. A disturbed wife,
>   instinctively, calls her working
>   husband to let him know to be
>   careful on the roads, saying:
>   "Honey be careful on the roads on
>   your way home, there's people
>   driving on the wrong side of the
>   road". The Husband sincerely
>   replies: "I KNOW, I AM PASSING
>   HUNDREDS OF THEM".

ANGEL CROSS, a blonde 30-something, White POLICE OFFICER, laughs and chuckles at THE CHIEF's little joke. ANGEL has bright blue eyes, like the sea.

MARTIN knocks...

>   THE CHIEF
>   (yells)
>   --MARTIN? That you?

                DETECTIVE MARTIN MALICE
         (from behind the
         door)
You know it, sir.

                THE CHIEF
--Come on in, meet your new
partner!

MALICE enters and shuts the door behind himself.

                ANGEL
         (reaches her hand
         out to shake
         MARTIN's)
--Hello, DETECTIVE MALICE, I've
heard many good things about you.

                DETECTIVE MARTIN MALICE
         (lets out a
         smelly-drunken
         burp)
--None great?--
         (doesn't shake
         ANGEL's hand)

                THE CHIEF
ANGEL CROSS meet MARTIN MALICE,
MARTIN meet---

                DETECTIVE MARTIN MALICE
--Cut the bullshit formalities,
CHIEF, I got this.
         (to ANGEL)
--Let's go Rookie.--

                ANGEL
I'm not a Rookie, sir. I've been a
cop for 8 years.

                DETECTIVE MARTIN MALICE
--Whatever Rookie, you're paying
for the coffee this morning...and
the breakfast.

                ANGEL
--Are you always this sexist?

                DETECTIVE MARTIN MALICE
--It would be sexist not to ask
you to buy us breakfast, you
know?--

                         THE CHIEF
          --You two go talk shit somewhere
          else...I'm busy here.

                    DETECTIVE MARTIN MALICE
          C'mon, ANGEL, we'll take my
          cruiser.

They exit the OFFICE, and subsequently the STATION.

                                        CUT TO:

INT. POLICE-CRUISER - MOMENTS LATER

The two cops ride through PC, it's quiet at first, MARTIN
tries to break the uncomfortable silence.

                    DETECTIVE MARTIN MALICE
          --Never trust a bald-barber. A
          Skinny Chef. Or a Lazy-eyed karate
          master...--

                         ANGEL
          --What do you mean?--

                    DETECTIVE MARTIN MALICE
          --DUALITY REIGNS...So where ya
          from, Rookie?

                         ANGEL
          --Here--PC. I was born here. I
          just moved back actually,
          transferred from the department in
          TEXAS. I grew up there, became a
          POLICE OFFICER, and then decided I
          wanted to come back to my roots.

                    DETECTIVE MARTIN MALICE
          --Why'd you become a cop?--

                         ANGEL
          --Why not? And, honestly, to clean
          the shit that needs to be
          cleaned...

                    DETECTIVE MARTIN MALICE
          Damn. I respect your truthfulness.
          Now, we're getting somewhere. I
          became a cop, hell, I guess I was
          a little younger than you, I
          became one to PROTECT AND
          SERVE...but, it kind of just went
          downhill as my career went
                         (MORE)

                    DETECTIVE MARTIN MALICE (cont'd)
forward. This job, kid, it ain't
what you think...when you get in
THE SHIT, you'll regret it every
other day after. And, trust me,
when the damage is done, it's
done. It just keeps coming too.
          (sighs, as ANGEL
           looks at him
           observantly)
Anyway, Denny's or McDonald's?

          ANGEL
--I'm vegan.--

          DETECTIVE MARTIN MALICE
--Well, well, a non-meat-eater,
huh?--Your brain will eat itself,
if you don't eat meat, true
protein, you know that right? They
use veganism in most cults...they
cut off their meat, and it
collapses their brain-functions as
the time passes, makes 'em easier
to control.

          ANGEL
--You really have no sense of
common-decency, do you?--

          DETECTIVE MARTIN MALICE
--I really don't. And, hell, don't
they have vegan at a Restaurant
around here?

          ANGEL
I'm going to just get coffee. I
ate before I left my house.

          DETECTIVE MARTIN MALICE
--Okay, you're still buyin' me
breakfast, Rookie...that's a
first-day rule.

          ANGEL
--It's not my first---

          DETECTIVE MARTIN MALICE
          (pulls into
          McDonald's)
I meant first day with me. I'm
gonna go in and grab my food. I
gotta use the bathroom too.

                                        CUT TO:

EXT. MCDONALD'S - CONTINUOUS

MALICE parks.

ANGEL gets out first, he waits a moment.

When she nears the entrance, MARTIN grabs his LIQUOR bottle
from out of the back, and he takes 3 massive swigs.

It calms his nerves, the nerve-juice. The coffee will perk
him back up.

                                        CUT TO:

INT. POLICE CRUISER - LATER

                    DETECTIVE MARTIN MALICE
               --Good God that was a
               good-breakfast, that coffee was
               superb.

                         ANGEL
                    (in awe of
                     MALICE's eating
                     abilities)
               --I've never seen a person eat
               that quick...and do you always
               drink on the job?

                    DETECTIVE MARTIN MALICE
                    (gets crazy-eyed)
               --This is America...you keep your
               fucking nose out of what I do,
               alright? Don't ever question me in
               regard to my sobriety, understood?

It gets uncomfortably silent.

The two cops ride down west 23rd street.

Out-of-the-blue a call comes in from the DISPATCHER.

                         DISPATCH
               All units, I repeat, all units, we
               have a robbery in progress at a
               convenient store at 225 West 23rd
               street. Please, respond.

                    DETECTIVE MARTIN MALICE
               (anticipatory)
          --10-4, DISPATCH, this is
          DETECTIVE MALICE, I'll take the
          call. I gotta Rookie that needs
          trainin'.

                                        CUT TO:

EXT. CONVENIENT-STORE - MOMENTS LATER

MALICE and ANGEL were only a couple of minutes away from the
robbery taking place.

He and she pull up to the scene right as the perpetrators
are leaving with the loot; only a couple hundred bucks...

MALICE parks, takes his pistol out the holster and proceeds
to exit the vehicle, ANGEL does the same.

                    DETECTIVE MARTIN MALICE
               (to the running
                perps)
          --Halt, or we will shoot!

The guys keep running.

                    DETECTIVE MARTIN MALICE
          Fire, ANGEL, now!

                    ANGEL
               (hesitates)
          -I--I Can't.

                    DETECTIVE MARTIN MALICE
               (aims steady yet
                still shaky from
                drinking)
          Fuck It.

The Detective shoots both men fatally with 4 shots.

Another THIEF comes out from inside the STORE with a shotgun
in-hand.

                    THIEF 1
               (dying)
          --Aah!!!--

                    THIEF 2
          --I--I
               (dies)

                        THIEF 3
                   (Shotgun pointed
                    at MALICE)
               You killed my brothers!!!

THIEF 3 pumps the shotgun as to fire.

                        ANGEL
                   (runs toward
                    MALICE)
               --NO!!!

ANGEL CROSS jumps in front of MARTIN and takes the
shotgun-blast to her chest, covered with a vest.

MARTIN MALICE blasts the THIEF away, unloading his weapon.

                   DETECTIVE MARTIN MALICE
                   (checking on ANGEL)
               -Dammit, girl, are you
               out-of-your-mind? Thank you for
               saving me, but don't ever do that
               again! Are you hurt?

                        ANGEL
                   (rips the vest
                    off, struggling
                    to breathe)
               --Goddammit!!! I'm good--I'm good.
               It just hurt me, it didn't go
               through though.

                   DETECTIVE MARTIN MALICE
                   (into his comms)
               --DISPATCH, I need paramedics,
               back-up, now! I have 3 dead perps.
               I have an OFFICER who's been hit!
                   (tends to ANGEL)
               --I'm not callin' you Rookie
               anymore. You're my Guardian Angel,
               huh?

                        ANGEL
                   (smiles painfully)
               --That's one way of lookin' at it,
               I guess, sir.

                   DETECTIVE MARTIN MALICE
                   (assisting ANGEL)
               Don't worry, help is coming.

                    ANGEL
          --You're not such an asshole after
          all.---You're just a douche, huh?

                    DETECTIVE MARTIN MALICE
          That shotgun blast made you a
          bitch, I'm guessing.

                    ANGEL
          Trust me, I'm always a bitch.

                    DETECTIVE MARTIN MALICE
          You saved me, why?

                    ANGEL
          I had to. I couldn't let you die.

                    DETECTIVE MARTIN MALICE
          Fair enough. Well, thank you. I
          could be bleeding on the concrete
          right now if you hadn't---

                    ANGEL
          --Don't sweat it. It's okay. We're
          good. Let's just proceed with our
          day. After I get seen, I'd like to
          do some work.

                    DETECTIVE MARTIN MALICE
          --You got it.--Why'd you hesitate?
          You wouldn't fire on those men,
          why?

                    ANGEL
          --In the eight years that I've
          been a cop, I've only fired my
          weapon 4 times. I've injured men,
          but---I refuse to kill them.

                    DETECTIVE MARTIN MALICE
          That kind of makes sense--well,
          ANGEL, here comes the Calvary.

Ambulances, police, the whole 9, begin arriving at the
scene.

                                        CUT TO:

INT. THE HOSPITAL - LATER

ANGEL lies on a hospital-bed, she's been admitted as there
is a massive bruise across her chest.

MARTIN is with her, he walks back in from the hallway after receiving a phone-call from THE CHIEF.

> DETECTIVE MARTIN MALICE
> --Thank you again, Rookie.

> ANGEL
> You said you wouldn't call me
> that...

> DETECTIVE MARTIN MALICE
> --I lied.---

MARTIN is smoking a cigarette inside the hospital. He doesn't care at all.

A nurse pokes her head in.

> NURSE
> --Sir! You cannot smoke in
> here!--Put out the cigarette, or
> leave, now!--

> DETECTIVE MARTIN MALICE
> (puffing cigarette
> smoke)
> --You mean You cannot smoke in
> here. You see this badge?
> (flips his badge)
> --This here reads that I can do
> whatever the fuck I want...now,
> you leave. I'm talking to my
> partner. I need some space.

The NURSE is shocked by MALICE's fiery words; he blows smoke in her face. She smacks her lips, but then leaves the room, no trouble.

> DETECTIVE MARTIN MALICE
> --Listen, I just got a call from
> the CHIEF, he needs me to go check
> out that murder-scene near the
> outskirts. I honestly forgot about
> it.-

> ANGEL
> (starts to get up)
> --I'll go with you, just let me--

> DETECTIVE MARTIN MALICE
> No, no. I got this. You've had
> enough fun for today. Who in the
> hell else gets shot on their first
> (MORE)

                    DETECTIVE MARTIN MALICE (cont'd)
day of transfer?

                    ANGEL
I guess you're right, I'll just
sit tight. It feels like Mike
Tyson punched me in my titties.
The spread missed almost pierced
my vest by a gnats eyebrow.

                    DETECTIVE MARTIN MALICE
          (laughs a bit)
Ha. Keep it between the ditches,
Rookie. I'll see ya probably
tomorrow. They said you'd be in
good shape by then. You'll be
working tomorrow I'm sure, they
just gotta do their medical thing
and what not. You know how that
paperwork goes.

                    ANGEL
Indeed, MALICE. Be careful out
there.

                    DETECTIVE MARTIN MALICE
          (exits the
           hospital room)
--Will do.--

                                   CUT TO:

INT. CRIME-SCENE #1 - DAY

MARTIN MALICE enters an abandoned HOUSE on the outskirts of
PANAMA CITY.

Many Forensic Investigators, police, various responders are
outside and inside the abandoned HOUSE.

MALICE walks in to a terrifying sight.

                    DETECTIVE MARTIN MALICE
          --How in God's
          Name---Impossible...

A WOMAN is hung by chains, upside down, a tub is underneath
her. The tub is full of coagulated blood. The WOMAN was
drained after having a mastectomy of torture. Her eye-balls
are filled with blood, red as a stop-sign.

MARTIN is shocked, because...he recognizes the WOMAN. He

recognizes the injuries, the blood. She's the woman that was in his dreams.

                    FORENSIC INVESTIGATOR 2
          Detective? You All Right?

MARTIN MALICE runs out of the house fast-as-a-bullet.

He vomits in the front yard, with his hands on his knees. The vomit smells of alcohol from yards away.

                    FORENSIC INVESTIGATOR 1
          --Get off the property, you
          dumb-fuck, you're contaminating
          the crime-scene!!!--

                                        CUT TO:

DETECTIVE MALICE charges to his vehicle, gets in, starts it, and takes off like the speed-racer.

He's more than unsettled, deeply disturbed beyond words.

                                        CUT TO:

INT. POLICE-CRUISER - MOMENTS LATER

MALICE is so erratic from seeing the dead female, that he grabs his bottle, and takes out the remainder of it in about 5 giant gulps.

He's drinking and driving, while completely distracted.

                    DETECTIVE MARTIN MALICE
          --W--What--How--Jesus Fuck!!!
               (sees the LIQUOR
                is gone)
          --I gotta get another bottle!

MALICE's phone starts ringing.

He answers, and tries to compose himself.

                    DETECTIVE MARTIN MALICE
               (into the phone)
          Hello?

                    DR. ALICIA
               (through the phone)
          --MR. MALICE, you have an
          appointment with me at 3:30. Will
          you be able to make it?

             DETECTIVE MARTIN MALICE
--Y--yes, Ma'am. I will be there
then. I actually--I need to talk
to someone, now.

             DR. ALICIA
        (through the phone)
My 2:00 cancelled, so you're more
than welcome to come buy now if
you like.

             DETECTIVE MARTIN MALICE
--I'm 15 minutes away. I'll be
there in 5...
        (hangs up)

                        CUT TO:

INT. THERAPY SESSION #23 - EVENING

In his THERAPY SESSION, MALICE talks to ALICIA...his
assigned psychologist. She is stunning, yet unassuming. Mid
30s, tall for a woman--she is White, has long brown hair and
near-black eyes.

THE CHIEF referred the detective to her after several
incidents on the job.

             DR. ALICIA
        (mid-discussion)
--FREEDOM is SELF-CONTROL, MR.
MALICE. You above all should know
that? You make choices, we all do.
But, you cannot allow yourself to
be trapped by those choices. It's
up to you, to free yourself,
through your free-will from the
bondage you feel. Your fear of
death is consuming you, you must
not let it.

             DETECTIVE MARTIN MALICE
--Do you know the definition of
MALICE, ALICIA?--

             DR. ALICIA
--Enlighten Me, MARTIN.--

             DETECTIVE MARTIN MALICE
--The intention, or desire to do
EVIL...that's what it means...

                    DR. ALICIA
--When you killed your last perp,
did you intend to? Do you go
around wanting to kill people as
an OFFICER OF THE LAW?

              DETECTIVE MARTIN MALICE
--No--I--The trouble always seems
to find me. I respond, react, and
then if I have to, I KILL. Like I
did today.--

                    DR. ALICIA
--There's a type-of DUALITY that
comes with your work, am I right?
You have to be able to balance
various things, aggression with
civility, power with politics,
pistols with paperwork...

              DETECTIVE MARTIN MALICE
--Yeah, that's about the gist of
it.

                    DR. ALICIA
What about repentance? Perhaps
that could help you with your
inner-turmoil--your guilt for
having killed...I sense it in you.
You feel badly about having taken
lives...

              DETECTIVE MARTIN MALICE
I'm not going to a mansion, to
confess to men who call themselves
"Papa" and they dress like Mama. I
ain't doing it. I'd rather--I grew
up Catholic. It ain't for me,
honey.

                    DR. ALICIA
--Understood.---Now, back to our
topic...Do you know the definition
of DUALITY???

              DETECTIVE MARTIN MALICE
--Hit me.

                    DR. ALICIA
--Two things of the same nature,
that contrast with one another,
yet are perfectly balanced.
Elegantly aligned.--The dual
nature of us all, it is quite
                    (MORE)

                    DR. ALICIA (cont'd)
beautiful. It's like--it's like
ORGANIZED CHAOS, all of our lives.
Do you understand what I mean by
that?

                    DETECTIVE MARTIN MALICE
--Absolutely. But--I must say,
with my alcohol problem, lack of
sleep, and my bad dreams, there's
no DUALITY to my life, or
organization...my life is pure
chaos.---

                    DR. ALICIA
--Perhaps you should voluntarily
admit yourself to
'LIFE-CONTROL'.--

                    DETECTIVE MARTIN MALICE
I'd be better off putting a
fucking bullet in my mouth...

                    DR. ALICIA
               (gets up from her
                chair)
--How about a Kiss instead?--

ALICIA kisses MARTIN MALICE, he kisses her back.

They proceed to make love in the "Therapy Session"...

                                        CUT TO:

INT. MARTIN'S HOME - NIGHT

MALICE sits alone in his HOME, simply sipping his liquor as
opposed to chugging.

                    DETECTIVE MARTIN MALICE
               (to himself)
--That fucking woman put a fucking
on me that ain't no going back
from.--

                                        CUT TO:

INT. DREAM-STATE - EVENING

The Sun is setting...

MARTIN and his WIFE are standing on a balcony off the coast, looking at the SUNSET...it's amazing, captivating beyond belief...

He is hugging her from behind.

She turns to face him.

                    MARTIN'S WIFE
          --MARTIN, never forget this
          moment. This moment in time. Let
          it last forever, I know I am.--

                    DETECTIVE MARTIN MALICE
                    (aware he's
                     dreaming and that
                     his wife is dead)
          --Honey, you're all I've ever
          known.
                    (crying, hugging
                     her tight)
          --What am I to do? What must I do
          to be with you again?--

She stands back a bit, and she's a different woman now.

She's a VICTIM...

Blood is spilling from her mouth, her tongue is gone, her teeth, her lips even...

                    VICTIM 2
                    (growling,
                     spitting blood
                     all over MALICE)
          --YOU MUST DIE!!!--

                    DETECTIVE MARTIN MALICE
                    (paralyzed by
                     utter fear)
          --Aah!!!--

                                        CUT TO:

INT. THE POLICE-STATION - MORNING

MALICE is in THE CHIEF's OFFICE, frantic, unraveled, unstable...

                    DETECTIVE MARTIN MALICE
                    (puts his badge on
                     the chief's desk)
          --I'm fucking done, CHIEF. I'm not
                    (MORE)

                    DETECTIVE MARTIN MALICE (cont'd)
cut out for this kinda work any
longer. I gotta cut it off at the
pass. I'm not going to another
fucking death-scene, I've seen too
much of it. I'm retiring, as of
right fucking now. So help me God.

                    THE CHIEF
               (stoic, doesn't
                give a shit)
--Yeah, yeah, I've heard this
spill a thousand times. You're
gonna need the help of God,
because, as you know, MARTIN,
you're our lead, LEAD,
homicide-Detective, you're our
guy, man. So, until those papers
are finalized, and if you want all
of your pension, then you will do
as you're told by me, and I say,
you go to that goddamn CRIME-SCENE
right now!!!

                    DETECTIVE MARTIN MALICE
--You--Ah, fuck it. You piece of
shit.
               (picks up his
                badge)

                    THE CHIEF
               (fiddles with his
                papers on his
                desk)
--Tell it to the mayor, ya
drunk...

                                        CUT TO:

ANGEL stands against a wall, posted up, waiting for MARTIN.

She greets him kindly, having healed properly and been
discharged an all.

                    ANGEL
--How's it hangin', sir?--

                    DETECTIVE MARTIN MALICE
--Hung and to the right...

                    ANGEL
--Dammit, I fell right into that
one. I meant "how are you doing?".
It came out wrong.--Anyway--Where
               (MORE)

                    ANGEL (cont'd)
to?

                DETECTIVE MARTIN MALICE
--Drive me to HIGHLAND VIEW.
There's a murder that took place
we gotta see about...

                    ANGEL
            (walking out the
             station with
             MARTIN)
Alrighty, so, you and the CHIEF
had a spat, huh?

                DETECTIVE MARTIN MALICE
--We fuss like a gay couple, don't
worry.

                              CUT TO:

INT. HIGHLAND VIEW HOME/CRIME-SCENE #2 - LATER

The Paramedics are bringing the murdered corpse out of the
abandoned house...

MALICE and ANGEL get out of the cruiser, just as the
responders move the body.

                DETECTIVE MARTIN MALICE
            (stops the
             paramedic)
        --What--What does her face look
        like?--

                    PARAMEDIC
--You don't wanna know,
DETECTIVE...Trust me.

MALICE pulls the bloodied sheet away, revealing the same
brutalized, mutilated face in his last dream.

He jumps back in pure panic.

                    ANGEL
        --What is it, sir? You've seen
        worse, right?

                    DETECTIVE MARTIN MALICE
          --I gotta go. ANGEL, hitch a ride.
          I---I gotta go see somebody right
          fucking now. I--I'll give you a
          call.

                    ANGEL
               (talking to the
                running MALICE,
                concerned)
          --O-okay, sir. Please, be careful.

MALICE leaves hastily from the CRIME-SCENE, it is all too
telling for him.

He's going to see his THERAPIST.

                                   CUT TO:

INT. THERAPY SESSION #24/UNANNOUNCED - LATER

MALICE bursts into ALICIA's session with another client.
He's out of breath, having an anxiety attack.

                    DR. ALICIA
          --Martin, you cannot be in here,
          right now. You are violating so
          many rights and laws, leave, now.

The client just sits quietly, shocked by MARTIN's startled
look.

                    DETECTIVE MARTIN MALICE
          --Doc, I just--I just need to
          talk--to you, please!

                    DR. ALICIA
          --Come back by tomorrow, as
          scheduled, MARTIN. I cannot see
          you today. I am sorry. If you
          can't wait till tomorrow to see
          me, then I can issue you a
          voluntary committal to the
          LIFE-CONTROL facility.

                    DETECTIVE MARTIN MALICE
          --I'm sorry too. I'll be back
          tomorrow. I shouldn't have come
          here. I'm sorry.

MARTIN stumbles out of the THERAPIST's office.

                              CUT TO:

INT. MARTIN'S HOME - MORNING

MALICE wakes up from his drunken rest...

He grabs the bottle, and chugs it a couple of times and goes
right back off to sleep...

                              CUT TO:

INT. DREAM STATE/FUNERAL - DAY

MALICE awakens at an unexpected place...

A FUNERAL, of all things.

He walks toward where the body is being buried, he sees the
people there watching, they do not see him. He has trouble
recognizing anyone, it's all fuzzy as he's in a DREAM STATE.

As MALICE walks up to the burial spot, he can see the casket
is still open...

A DEAD WOMAN reaches her hand out of the grave and grabs
MALICE by the foot; he collapses backward and lands on his
back.

The DEAD WOMAN jumps out of the grave, and claws her way to
MARTIN...

He tries to evade, to no avail.

                    DEAD WOMAN
                 (demonic
                  voice-tone)
            --You Did This!!! Now, I'll take
            You to The Grave!!!---

                    DETECTIVE MARTIN MALICE
            --Holy Hell, IT'S YOU!!!--

                    DEAD WOMAN
                 (grabs MALICE by
                  the throat, roars)
            --Yes, Me, Me, Me!!!---

She snaps MARTIN's neck like a twig...

                              CUT TO:

INT. MARTIN'S HOME - CONTINUOUS

MARTIN flails awake, he felt the pain inflicted in his dream...

The distraught detective grabs his gun, badge, and his bottle, and proceeds to leave his residence.

He's going back to that place, his first kill...

                                        CUT TO:

EXT. PANAMA CITY NEIGHBORHOOD - LATER

MARTIN MALICE rushes through the NEIGHBORHOOD.

To him, it is awfully familiar.

Spontaneously, he sees a naked woman, covered in blood, running in the road toward him.

                    VICTIM 3
                (at the
                 top-of-her-lungs,
                 yet struggling to
                 speak)
            --Aah!!! HELP ME!!! Please,
            somebody do something!!!--

The DETECTIVE pulls about 10 ft from the VICTIM, and he parks, gets out and sees about her.

                    DETECTIVE MARTIN MALICE
                (assisting the
                 VICTIM as best he
                 can)
            --Miss?! Are you alright?! Where
            are you hurt?!--

                    VICTIM 3
                (turns around)
            --EVERYWHERE!!!---

When the VICTIM turns around, MARTIN MALICE sees that she has a scar all-the-way from her belly-button to her throat...

Some of her Organs have been removed. It takes all of her energy just to speak. She is in a CHAOTIC state...

MALICE tries to comfort the VICTIM, she sees him and falls flat on her back, concussively hitting her head. She is dying in MARTIN's arms...

The DETECTIVE immediately calls his partner.

>   ANGEL
>   (through the phone)
>   Yes, boss? What's up?

>   DETECTIVE MARTIN MALICE
>   (soberly)
>   --L--listen, Angel, get to
>   GULF-VIEW, now! I got a woman here
>   in real bad shape, she's dying! I
>   need first-responders, the whole
>   nine! Alright?!

>   ANGEL
>   --I'm on the way, I'm only a few
>   minutes from there. Sit tight,
>   sir, help is on the way.---

>   DETECTIVE MARTIN MALICE
>   --O--okay, I'm gonna try to
>   resuscitate the VICTIM--
>   (hangs up)
>   Fuck!
>   (tries to revive
>   the girl)
>   --DON'T YOU DIE ON ME!!!--

The VICTIM comes to.

She points to one of the houses, only 30 yards or so away
from MALICE.

>   VICTIM 3
>   --She--She is waiting for you...
>   (succumbs to death)

>   DETECTIVE MARTIN MALICE
>   (keeps trying to
>   save the girl
>   with
>   mouth-to-mouth)
>   Who? Who is waiting for me?

The VICTIM is dead.

MARTIN discontinues trying to bring her back.

                    DETECTIVE MARTIN MALICE
                        (to himself)
            --Why didn't I see this one in my
            dreams?--I could've stopped it...

MALICE stumbles to his car, opens the door, and grabs the
LIQUOR out of the vehicle. He takes 5 massive gulps straight
from the big bottle...

He's dumbfounded and downtrodden by the sight of another
corpse...

No one comes out of their homes to assist MARTIN. It's
eerily silent in the NEIGHBORHOOD.

                    DETECTIVE MARTIN MALICE
            --I gotta see what's in that
            house. I just gotta.

The stubborn DETECTIVE proceeds to the house that VICTIM 3
was pointing to.

The Door is cracked.

There is a heavy stench of not only death, but also of
familiarity to MARTIN MALICE. The house reminds the drunkard
of a time before; a terrible time, forgotten.

                                        CUT TO:

MARTIN enters the house, and shuts the door.

INT. HOUSE - MOMENTS LATER

DETECTIVE MALICE proceeds with caution.

He is drunk now. He unbuckles his holster, and draws his
weapon, shaking as he does it...

He hears the screams of a woman, like, the sound of torture
occurring. As he moves toward the roars of pain, they get
quieter.

He gets to a door after moving through the hallway.

The door he opens leads to the basement, to a sight he can't
believe with his own two eyes.

                    DETECTIVE MARTIN MALICE
            --What the fuck are you doing
            here? What is all this?

MARTIN sees bodies strung up with chains by their feet. All
WOMEN...

The floor is laden with thick, coagulated-blood...

MALICE walks down the steps with his Gun pointed
at...ALICIA.

ALICIA is there, and she is drenched in blood, standing
behind a surgical-table. The table that VICTIM 3 was on
before "escaping".

                    DETECTIVE MARTIN MALICE
                 (prepared to shoot)
          --ALICIA?! Why? You're the
          Killer?--

                    DR. ALICIA
          --I let that WOMAN go just hoping
          she'd distract you and direct you
          to me at the same-time, in
          cinematic fashion. It's so
          thrilling isn't it? I've completed
          my work, with you here now. You're
          the last piece of the puzzle,
          MARTIN...

                    DETECTIVE MARTIN MALICE
          --Put your hands on your head, and
          put your knees on the ground!
          You're under-arrest, you have the
          right to remain silent---

                    ANGEL
                 (from behind
                 MALICE)
          --I got your six, partner.--

MARTIN is somewhat relieved that back-up has arrived.

                    DR. ALICIA
          --MARTIN, all the love we made,
          and now you treat me like a
          common-crook?--

                    DETECTIVE MARTIN MALICE
                 (to ALICIA)
          --You know nothing of love, my
          dear.
                 (to ANGEL)
          --Cuff her, ANGEL, put her in my
          vehicle.

                    ANGEL
               (goes to cuff
                ALICIA)
          --There's a lot of bodies here,
          boss. What's the next step?

MARTIN turns around, he hears no sign of help.

                    DETECTIVE MARTIN MALICE
               (notices that it's
                still silent
                around him)
          --Where the hell are the
          paramedics, where's the back-up,
          ANGEL?

MARTIN starts to walk up the stairs...

                    ANGEL
          --They died slow, these people...

                    DETECTIVE MARTIN MALICE
          --How can you tell?--

                    ANGEL
          --BECAUSE, I HELPED KILL THEM--

ANGEL CORTEZ, faster than a gun-slinger, shoots MARTIN
MALICE in the back.

He falls down the stairs to the basement floor, badly
injured.

ANGEL CORTEZ un-cuffs her sister, ALICIA.

                    DETECTIVE MARTIN MALICE
               (in utter
                disbelief)
          You--You bitches! Why?!

                    DR. ALICIA
          --The day you killed our mother in
          front of us--

                    ANGEL
          --We swore we'd take your life
          from you, and here we are,
          DETECTIVE. You're at the end,
          drunk, defeated, destined to
          die...

                    DETECTIVE MARTIN MALICE
          --The bodies, you killed all those
          people...you--

                    DR. ALICIA
          --We enjoy killing. Women,
          especially. You're the only man
          that we will have killed, so far,
          anyway. And, we're gonna make it
          quick. Eye for an eye. You killed
          our mother with a gun, that's how
          you die.

                    DETECTIVE MARTIN MALICE
          --Y--You two are the daughters of
          ANGELA. ANGELA CORTEZ...

                    ANGEL
          --So you do remember her, even as
          drunk as you are?

MARTIN draws his weapon and goes to fire.

The fire-arm fails to fire, it's empty...

                    ANGEL
          --Who's the Rookie, now...Sir?---

                    DR. ALICIA
                 (smirking, wiping
                  her bloody hands
                  off with a
                  white-towel)
          --ANGEL, please put the DETECTIVE
          out of his misery. He need not
          feel it any longer.--

                    ANGEL
          --This is for my Mama--See You in
          Hell, MALICE...

                    DETECTIVE MARTIN MALICE
          --DEATH cancels everything but
          TRUTH.--

                    DR. ALICIA
          --What are Words to a 'Ruger'?---

ANGEL pulls her Glock, and walks right up to MALICE.

She unloads the weapon into him.

He DIES, dead-as-a-doornail.

Revenge is tasty for the young Serial-Killing-Sisters...

                    DR. ALICIA
               (hugs her sister)
          --Good Work, Sis. My ANGEL.--Mama
          would be proud of us.

                    ANGEL
               (hugs her ALICIA
                tighter)

The SISTERS stand around the bodies, in the bloody-mess,
hugging with solace and peace, knowing their perceived
tormentor has bit-the-bullets, quite literally.

Death's hand ascends to take MALICE's soul back to the
dust...

Hell hath no Fury like two sisters scorned...

ANGEL and ALICIA..."THE RIPPER SISTERS" as they're to be
known as...

TO BE CONTINUED...

                                        FADE OUT.

Brandon S. Todd

Printed in the United States
By Bookmasters